You Again

VAL TOBIN

DEDICATION

To my readers, thank you. To Bob, Jenn, Mark,
Chanelle, Savannah, and Jack, always.

ACKNOWLEDGMENTS

Thank you to Jenn Cunningham; members of the Legal Fiction group; Carol Frank; Melanie Smith; Kelly Tomlinson; Alis B. Kennedy; Wendy Quirion; Val Cseh; John Erwin; Michelle Legere; Pat Folliott; and Diane King for beta reading, professional advice, and suggestions.
Editing by Kelly Hartigan (XterraWeb) editing.xterraweb.com. Thank you, Kelly.
Thanks to Patti Roberts of Paradox (paradoxbooktrailerproductions.blogspot.com.au/) for the amazing cover and for asking me to contribute to your series.

CHAPTER 1

Gretchen Brown, the personnel manager at By the Books Accounting, poked her head into Ellen Haddigan's cubicle. Without stepping inside, she reached in and set a small, wrapped package on Ellen's desk.

"Happy birthday. Don't tell anyone," she whispered and disappeared again.

Ellen took a moment to bury her head in her hands and groan silently.

Birthdays. They revealed so much: age, size of social circle, and obligations. The age part didn't bother Ellen, who, on her thirtieth birthday, sat at her desk working on a client's financials. What did she care if people knew her age? She heartily believed in the saying that age is just a number.

The size of her social circle wasn't important either. She preferred a smaller group to call good friends but also enjoyed large crowds of strangers. Rhonda Miller, who owned an art gallery in Yorkville, fulfilled the role of best friend, and Ellen loved having only one close female friend. She could depend on Rhonda, and Rhonda could depend on Ellen. So, no, age and a small social circle didn't bother her.

The obligations associated with birthdays—and Christmas, Easter, and Valentine's Day—were what made her cringe. She'd have to remember every person who wished her a happy birthday today, every person who gave her a gift, and every person who made a thoughtful gesture. Each show of generosity meant she'd have to reciprocate on their special day, and that took too much work and thought. Why couldn't people be practical and refuse to participate in these meaningless traditions? They'd save thousands of dollars and megatons of stress.

Yet, the closer it got to lunchtime in the small accounting company for which she worked, the closer it came to Cake Time. This tradition impacted everyone equally, and there was a strict no-gifts rule.

Whenever an employee had a birthday, the company sprang for a cake. She supposed it boosted morale, but for her, it brought the dreaded obligations. And despite the rule, someone always bought her a gift and slipped it to her before the end of the day—as Gretchen most recently evidenced. The personnel manager had broken her own rule.

During the almost three years Ellen had worked here, the single gift she'd received after the first birthday celebration they'd held for her had exploded into three gifts received so far today, and the day wasn't anywhere near over yet. The gifts brought the obligations. The sense of obligation brought guilt.

No one else she knew had a problem with this stuff. Sometimes, she considered talking to a therapist about it, but she'd never followed through on the impulse. If this was her only neurosis, she could live with it. No one else knew she was so petty and selfish. No one else knew she was so logical and practical. She hid it well, except from Rhonda, who'd heard numerous tipsy diatribes from Ellen on the stupidity of gift-giving and silly social obligations.

The time at the bottom right of her computer changed to 12:00 p.m., and chairs shifted away from desks in the cubicles around her. Ellen sighed and rose from her chair. She pasted a smile on her face as her head popped prairie dog-like above the partition, and coworkers straggled past her to the kitchen. Cake Time had arrived.

They gathered in the company kitchen. Gretchen, the official cake lady, already stood next to the kitchen table. The cake, a vanilla sheet cake with vanilla buttercream frosting and guaranteed nut-free, sat atop the table. Two candles, one shaped like the number three and the other a zero, stuck out of the middle of the cake. Around them scrawled the words *Happy Birthday Ellen* in a fancy curlicue script.

The group huddled around the table, leaving the middle spot, the place of honour in front of the cake, vacant for Ellen. She dutifully assumed the position. Gretchen lit the candles, sucked in a breath, and led them all in a rousing chorus of "Happy Birthday."

When that was done, Ellen picked up the knife Gretchen had set next to the cake and carefully cut the large block into pieces. She scooped enough pieces onto the paper plates provided so that everyone who wanted a piece received one. The kitchen slowly cleared out as each employee went about their lunchtime business, taking slices of cake back to their desks to eat at their leisure.

Ellen poured herself coffee from the urn, doctored it with milk and sugar, and carried her coffee and cake back to her desk. What remained of the cake she left on the kitchen table for anyone who wanted seconds.

This was another small resentment Ellen held: these cake days destroyed her diet. Not only would she have to skip lunch to eat this dessert, but she'd have seconds, and that would pile calories on to whatever she'd have for dinner. She could skip the cake, but who could resist cake? No, she'd eat it, and she'd hate herself for it. Cake days, and other days where treats appeared in the office, made the last ten pounds she wanted to lose impossible.

Back at her desk, she set her travel mug and plate next to her monitor. While most of her coworkers left the building for lunch, Ellen preferred to eat at her desk. She savoured the peace and quiet of an empty office and took this time to read or surf the net.

Today, she poked around on her favourite online fashion site, her cart filled with a hot pair of fashion boots, a cape—who couldn't use a cape?—and a flouncy skirt she could see herself wearing with the boots.

As her hand hovered over the "Checkout" button, her office email alert dinged, and she couldn't resist peeking at who sent the message: Carol Frank, the accounting director and Ellen's boss. The subject read *Morning Meeting*. The pit of Ellen's stomach knotted. There'd been no meeting this morning, so the message referred to the following morning. Ellen opened the email, and sure enough, Carol requested her presence in her office first thing next morning.

Ellen scowled. This could only be about a new client. Her caseload was already full. One more would squeeze her, especially at tax time.

I can use the overtime, she consoled herself, clicking "Checkout" and shoving a large forkful of cake into her mouth.

***

The rest of the day passed both quickly and uneventfully. More relieved than usual when five o'clock arrived, Ellen packed the three small gifts she'd received that day into her purse and headed to the elevator. Rhonda had already texted to say she was waiting at the tavern down the street.

By the Books was located in a twenty-storey office building on Bloor Street in Toronto's Bloor-Yorkville area. Surrounded by upscale shops, boutiques, restaurants, hotels, and galleries, the location provided easy access to public transportation and anything Ellen wanted. When she arrived at the Foundation Saloon, it was already dark outside though it was only 5:40 p.m.

She stepped into the chandelier-lit warmth of the entryway, grateful to be out of the bitter November cold. It hadn't snowed yet this year, but it was coming. The clouds and sky loomed grey and heavy. The hostess greeted her, and when Ellen gave her name, the woman nodded in recognition and directed her to follow.

Ellen spotted Rhonda's smooth brunette cap of hair and round cherub face immediately. She sat at the bar, which replicated the bar and barstools of an old-fashioned western saloon. Double swinging doors at the bar's entrance solidified the theme. The aroma of chicken wings and fries made Ellen's stomach rumble, reminding her she'd had only two pieces of cake to eat all day.

When she recognized Ellen, Rhonda lifted a martini glass and its cherry-red contents in greeting. After telling the hostess she'd spotted her friend, Ellen wound her way through the crowded bar tables and high-backed chairs with quick, long-legged strides.

"We're sitting at the bar?" she asked when she reached her destination.

"You said keep it casual," Rhonda replied as Ellen eased onto a stool.

"Sure. This'll be fine." The stools had backs, and the music wasn't so loud they had to scream at each other. She liked the ambience here. It was active and energizing.

As they chatted, her gaze drew constantly to the mirror behind the bar, which reflected both women in a flattering light. She shook her head, letting her light-brown curls cascade off her shoulders and down her back.

Rhonda laughed. "You look great. The cold put colour into those pale cheeks of yours, and your hair has that sexy windblown look."

Ellen blushed. "It's silly. I've been feeling as if I should be somewhere else in my life right now."

"You mean other than out for drinks with me?"

"No. I mean ... I don't know what I mean." But she did, so that was a lie. She'd thrown away three good years by jumping ship from her last workplace, but it hadn't been her fault. She'd had to get away from that place. After what happened with Gabriel Duncan—no, she wouldn't think about that now. The whole debacle had cost her a job, an apartment ...

Rhonda interrupted Ellen's musings. "I have something for you."

When Ellen's head snapped around and her eyes blazed, Rhonda chuckled. "Relax. It doesn't mean you have to get me anything for my birthday. I saw it and thought of you. I'd have bought it regardless." She handed Ellen a small, wrapped box.

Ellen accepted it with a smile and a thanks and peeled off the paper. She removed the lid from what was obviously a jewellery box and peered inside to find a bracelet with pink stones in a silver setting.

"It's beautiful." She gave Rhonda a puzzled look.

"The quartz stones represent the heart chakra, but I bought pink instead of green to encourage romantic love."

"Why did you think of me for this? And what's a chakra?" Ellen asked, genuinely puzzled.

Rhonda tilted her head to the side as she contemplated. "It'll provide energetic healing, working on all levels to encourage romance—something you could use after the last few years you've had. And it's pretty. I thought it would look nice on you. Chakras are energy centres in the body. Seven different chakra centres exist, but I focused on the heart."

"Well, thanks again. It's lovely." Ellen wasn't into all the new age stuff Rhonda loved, but the bracelet was unique and pretty, so she'd wear it happily. She set the box on the bar and picked up the trinket. She wrapped the bracelet around her left wrist. After gently snapping the clasp closed, she held her arm out so she could admire the pink and silver decorating the soft cotton of her shirtsleeve.

"It's gorgeous against this black," she commented.

The bartender, who'd been fixing two cocktails in front of them, handed the drinks to the women. He nodded his head at a nearby table. "Compliments of the two gentlemen over there."

Rhonda's face broke into a bright smile. She turned toward the men, held up her hand, and wiggled her fingers at them. Ellen motioned to do the same but reined in her enthusiasm as thoughts of her one passionate night with Gabriel Duncan intruded. More to the point, she flashed back to what came after that one night, and she cringed. She acknowledged the men's gesture with a polite nod.

Both men waved the women over.

CHAPTER 2

"See? Your bracelet is working already. Let's join them." Rhonda started to slide off her barstool.

Ellen caught her arm. "We're here to celebrate my birthday."

"How better than to have drinks with two good-looking men?"

Rhonda was right: both men were attractive, and they appeared successful. Each wore a tailored suit and oozed confidence. The dark one sported a rugged hint of scruff under his nose and on his chin. The pale blond was clean-shaven but with a nicely contoured face and bright blue eyes.

"They look as if they visit the spa more than I do," Ellen said, "and that's tough to beat. I go at least once a month."

"So what? I like a guy who cares about his looks. I like a woman who cares about her looks—that's why we're friends. Come on. They're waiting."

When Ellen slipped from her chair, Rhonda, carrying her drink, went ahead and sat at the table with the two men. Ellen followed more slowly, sipping from her drink as she walked. It helped brace her, and by the time she arrived at the seat they'd pulled out for her, her nerves had steadied. Thoughts of Gabriel Duncan evaporated, and she smiled at the men as she introduced herself and Rhonda.

The blond led the conversation. He introduced himself as John Aylmer and his friend as Max Gorham. Both worked as lawyers and had offices in Yorkville. John handled labour-related cases, and Max was a prosecuting attorney. They seemed nice, and though Ellen kept one hand over her drink while she had anything in her glass, she relaxed enough to enjoy herself. Perhaps she'd start dating again, give men another chance. The prospect of that terrified her, but she had to get over this fear of getting hurt.

Yet she had such good reason. Gabriel had made her believe—it didn't matter. He was out of her life and had been for the last three years. Ever since that night. She'd promised herself she wouldn't dwell on the past tonight. Then again, tonight was supposed to be about celebrating with her friend, not with men.

Rhonda, at least, seemed to be thoroughly enjoying herself, and sparks were evident between her and Max. They'd drawn their chairs closer together and bantered and flirted outrageously. Each laughed at the other's little jokes as if they'd known one another for years.

Ellen watched Max closely, making sure he didn't slip anything into Rhonda's drink while she wasn't looking, but he never even glanced at her glass. His gaze remained fixed on Rhonda's eyes, her lips, and occasionally her breasts.

Of course he's watching her boobs. He's a guy and her boobs are spectacular. Even I glance at them when I talk to her.

"So, you're a bookkeeper." John at least sounded interested when he said it, but he was just making polite small talk.

"Accounting tech. Not an exciting job, but it keeps me employed. Do you live around here?"

"I've got a condo on Lake Shore. You?"

She regretted asking him now. Lake Shore Boulevard was an impressive location. His condo would overlook Lake Ontario, and many of the properties there were pricey and coveted. Now that he'd asked, she'd have to tell him she lived with her parents. Or did she? Why? He was a stranger, and she didn't plan to see him again.

"I live in Rosedale." There. That was a compromise. She gave the chichi location without telling him it wasn't hers.

"Nice." He glanced at her empty glass. "Care for another?"

"Sure." She glanced at Rhonda and Max, who now sat so close to one another they might have fused together. Obviously, her friend had settled in for the evening. "How 'bout I order some wings or something?" she suggested. "Have you eaten?"

"I'll get it."

"No, please, allow me." No way would she let him pay for everything. He'd bought the drinks. She refused to let him pay for anything else.

He accepted her offer with a grin, and the rest of the night passed pleasantly enough for Ellen to leave the restaurant happy she'd accepted the drinks and the company. Rhonda left with Max's phone number, and she'd given him hers as well—her real one. Ellen and John simply bid one another goodnight and nice meeting you.

11

On their cab ride home, Ellen gave her friend a sly grin. "You and Max got along well."

"We did, didn't we?" Rhonda replied.

"Let's look him up online," Ellen suggested, pulling her cell phone from her purse.

Rhonda giggled. "I already did," she whispered.

Ellen laughed. "You did? When?"

"When we went to the bathroom—after we ate the food you ordered. You were in the stall. I had a minute or two to kill, so I checked him out. He's a partner in his firm." Her voice held wonder and a small measure of pride. "Had his name in the paper too. He handled some big-name cases."

"Well, I guess that bodes well, but you should still be cautious. Serial killers can come from anywhere."

Rhonda scowled. "For God's sake, Ellen, he's not a serial killer."

"No, probably not. You plan to see him again, don't you?"

"Yes. He's a catch. We got along great, and I'm attracted to him. Why wouldn't I see him again? How do you think people become couples?"

"Did you verify he's not married?"

"He's not. That was the first thing I checked."

"Okay. That's a good start. Do you know how old he is? How come he's not married? Is he at least divorced? He seems too old to have never had a serious relationship."

"I don't know everything yet. Don't worry. I'll find out. And when we go out, we'll meet in a public place." She frowned. "I've never married either."

"Okay, but let me know when you go out, and give me the details of everywhere you'll be, and text me when you get home."

"No problem." Rhonda didn't blink at the commands. Most female friends looked out for one another this way. It was a life-and-death matter.

They reached Rhonda's condominium apartment building, and she paid her part of the fare. The women said their goodbyes, and as Rhonda stepped from the car, she said, "Thanks for a wonderful evening. Happy birthday. And Ellen, just because I'm willing to take a chance, it doesn't mean I'm taking a risk. I can still be cautious. Think about that."

***

Ellen's mother, Joanne, greeted Ellen when she stepped into the house through the back door, which provided a separate entrance to her basement apartment. Joanne had the door to the main floor open at the top of the stairs and stood there, hands on hips and frown on face. She wore a fluffy pink housecoat over her pyjamas, giving her plump figure extra padding. Cinched at the waist with a long belt, the ensemble made her resemble a pink Care Bear. Her blonde hair was tied into two long braids and wrapped around her head.

"You're so late on a weeknight."

"Hi, Mom. It's ten o'clock."

"I don't want to be a nag, dear, but you have work in the morning." Joanne's Scottish accent grew thicker whenever she was upset, worried, tired—in other words, anything but calm and well rested.

"Then don't be." Ellen cursed herself inside for the snarky remark. Her mother could make her behave childishly faster than anyone else alive. "Sorry," she amended. "Rhonda took me out for birthday drinks. I told you she would this morning when I left."

"Yes, but I didn't think you'd be this late. I baked you a birthday cake."

Guilt washed over Ellen. "I didn't know."

"I always make you a birthday cake." Joanne's sour expression morphed into a pout.

"Yes, but we don't always have it on my birthday. We get together for dinner on a Sunday, when Dad's likely to be home."

"When you weren't living here. Now, I thought we'd celebrate on your birthday."

The argument had become tiring, as any argument with her mother tended to do, and Ellen dropped the subject. She didn't feel like cake at ten o'clock at night, and it would be even later by the time she washed up and put her PJs on, but she didn't want to disappoint her mother further. Her father was away on business. Perhaps that was why Joanne had anticipated Ellen's homecoming so much tonight. She was probably just lonely. Ellen vowed to remain pleasant no matter how much her mother goaded her.

"Sorry I wasn't home earlier. Let me get changed. I'll come up and make tea, and we'll have the cake. Would that suit you?"

It did.

After Ellen changed into soft, comfy loungewear, she went upstairs to her mother's and the two sat at the kitchen table, cups of tea before them, the teapot between them. The cake, two slices missing, sat next to the teapot.

Her mother had gone all out. She'd baked a mint chocolate layer cake with mint chocolate frosting. Each bite Ellen took settled itself atop the wings and fries in her stomach, but nothing tasted as delectable going down as mint chocolate fudge. She figured this would cost a zillion calories.

"Oh, I can't believe I almost forgot!" Joanne jumped from her chair and hurried from the kitchen. "Don't move—I'll be right back," she hollered from somewhere in the living room.

She returned with an envelope in her hand. She beamed a smile at Ellen and handed her the card. "Happy birthday."

Ellen groaned inwardly. She'd told her mother not to get her anything. Instead of reminding her, though, she smiled and said, "Thanks so much, Mom."

She tore open the envelope and removed the card. Inside it, she found a gift card for a half-day of pampering for two at a nearby spa. She thought of Rhonda but immediately dismissed the idea. How long had it been since she'd spent quality time with her mother? This way, she wouldn't feel so obligated over accepting the gift since her mother would use it too.

"Thank you. Let's go together."

Joanne's face lit up with such delight Ellen felt relief and gratitude at the decision.

"We'll set it up for the weekend, okay?" Ellen suggested.

"Book it for Saturday," Joanne replied. "In the morning. Your dad and I are having people over for cocktails, and you'll want to look your best. You have to be there."

"Oh, Mother, what have you done?" Ellen's heart sank. This gathering must be another ploy to find Ellen a husband whether or not she wanted one.

"Nothing, dear. We've invited some friends over— and their kids. Well, kids your age."

Ellen shook her head. "Let me guess: most of them

have sons my age."

"Well, it doesn't hurt to meet them now, does it?"

"Not at all. But I'm not interested in sparking up a relationship with anyone, so don't put your matchmaker hat on."

"I wouldn't dream of it." Joanne smiled, and it was more than a little self-satisfied.

CHAPTER 3

Ellen jolted from bed, her cell phone tinkling the alarm for—Ellen glanced at the time—at least ten minutes, and she'd set it to go off with only minutes to spare. She hurried to the bathroom, which was next to the kitchen, almost tripping over Mister Cuddles, her tabby cat, in her scramble to get there.

Once out of the bathroom, she flipped on her television to catch the morning traffic report, one eye on the current time. She slowed her pace when she realized she'd gotten through the morning wash-up faster than she'd ever done. Yanking a navy blazer and dress pants from her closet, she dropped them on the bed and hunted out a white turtleneck.

The bracelet Rhonda had given her sat on the top of her dresser. Should she wear it to work? Would everyone think she was some kind of pagan?

She considered for a few moments and put it on. Most people would think it was pretty stones and wouldn't attribute any significance to it. The trinket was beautiful. She wasn't ashamed of it. Some clients

17

or coworkers might not appreciate Rhonda's beliefs, but they wouldn't suspect its new age properties simply by looking at the bracelet.

As Ellen dressed, she continued to glance at the television. The traffic had finished, and all seemed well on the streets she'd take to work. If she skipped breakfast, she'd catch the usual bus and make it to the subway that would let her out close to work with plenty of time to spare. She'd have enough time to grab a coffee and muffin before that meeting with her boss. From the closet, she took out a pair of high-heeled beige pumps. No snow on the sidewalks yet, so she could get away with shoes. She checked the time again.

Time to leave. She slipped on the shoes and moved to turn off the television.

Something the newscaster said caught her attention. She stopped fiddling with the remote and tuned in.

"... Duncan Technologies may have saved a floundering company when they closed a deal three weeks ago and purchased Business Reports Inc. Gabriel Duncan, son of Charles Duncan, assumed the role of company president.

"This latest purchase brings the total to three companies this year, in different parts of the world, with another soon to close in London. All are tech companies that specialize in business development and reporting software. Gabriel Duncan will take over as president for this newest acquisition. Back in Toronto, only a year after spending the previous two years at a branch in London, England, Duncan reportedly plans to expand the new business, which, without this takeover, would've likely gone under.

"In fashion news—"

Ellen pressed the power button, cutting off the rest.

Normally, she'd have been riveted to the screen over the latest news in fashion, but as she'd listened to the announcement about Gabriel, she'd grown nauseated. She needed to shut down the messenger of that horrifying news before she threw up or passed out.

He's back in Toronto. If she had asthma, she'd be reaching for an inhaler.

Based on the news report, he now had more responsibility in his father's company and had bought the company for which she'd once worked. The news of BRI's probable demise without Gabriel's intervention gave her more pause than the news that the man who'd broken her heart was back in the city.

While she'd worked at BRI, the company had prospered. Gabriel frequented the place as a client because his father's company hired them for overflow work. If they were in trouble, it perhaps made sense Duncan Technologies would want to buy them out. They likely expected to turn the situation around quickly and would also continue to have access to the developers there.

Thank God, she'd left when she did. Had she stayed, she'd be forced to either work with Gabriel or leave—an easy decision. She wanted to ensure she'd never see him again—even if the risk of that was already almost nil. Everything about the place reminded her of him and their time together. She'd grieved as if she'd lost a soul mate, which she'd thought he was. Rhonda's new age beliefs about the existence of soul mates had influenced Ellen more than she'd realized until Gabriel had shattered the delusion when he abandoned her for the sake of his career.

She picked up her purse, shaking off the thoughts of Gabriel as she had countless times in the last three years. When, oh, when, would she stop reliving the after-effects of that night? The night itself, in her eyes, had been spectacular, and she re-experienced it as she picked up her purse and headed out the door despite her resolve to stop thinking about him.

She'd been working late on BRI's taxes—at tax time, she often worked late especially on a Friday night when she wanted to get as much done before the start of the weekend as possible. Gabriel dropped by the office to review some software functionality BRI coders had added to a piece of reporting software they'd created for Duncan Tech. He was still there when she packed it up and left for the day, and when he saw her leaving, he suggested they go for a drink at a nearby bar. She agreed.

He'd attracted her for months—ever since she'd laid eyes on him the first time he'd walked through their doors. His looks drew her. He had a trim but muscular physique and wore expensive suits that exuded success and class. At six-foot-something, he towered over her five-foot-eight-inches, but the discrepancy was perfect. She could wear heels and still feel normal next to him.

His pretty-boy face gave him a youthful appearance, and his brown eyes always sparkled, making him seem as if he were not just happy with life but also thrilled with everything he did and everyone he met. Every time he saw her, those eyes lit up and his lush, sculpted lips grinned with pleasure. When they talked, he frequently touched her arm in a gentle but intimate manner. She responded to him in kind.

Whenever she spotted him, a thrill warmed her, and when his fingers brushed her arm or patted her hand, a spark of electrical attraction jolted through her. On days she didn't see him, she missed him with an ache she could barely stand. Anytime he visited, he brought coffee and baked goods for the office staff, but he hand-delivered her a cup of coffee and a special treat to her desk. He took her out for lunch once a month, and she enjoyed and savoured those jaunts. They laughed, chatted, and had fun. No one could've faulted her for thinking the attraction was mutual.

That Friday, when he suggested they go to a bar, she could barely contain her excitement. They would finally start seeing each other outside the office; she was certain of it. Drinks would turn into dinner. Dinner would turn into something more. She planned to invite him back to her apartment. At the time, she had a small condo at Dundas and Yonge, overlooking the Eaton Centre. It wasn't the penthouse, but it was quaint, it was hers, and she was proud of it—proud enough to let an obviously wealthy man with class and taste into it.

Part one of her plan worked smashingly.

Gabriel treated her to dinner after they had a couple of drinks, and it was obvious neither wanted the night to end. Over coffee and dessert, ordered more to extend the evening than because they were still hungry, she invited him to her apartment. The invitation in her suggestion was clear: she wanted him to spend the night. He was eager, willing. He said yes despite having to catch a plane to London the next day.

The moment they stepped over the threshold into her apartment unit, she tossed her purse to the floor, and they crashed together in a heated embrace. The July evening had been hot, but the chill from the air conditioner didn't dampen the fire flaming their passion.

She wrapped her legs around his thighs, and he carried her into the bedroom. Neither spoke. Neither had to. He paused long enough to slip on a condom, but the first time they made love, they never removed all their clothes—only what was necessary to get the job done in a frenzy of lust and desire.

As Ellen relived each thrilling touch on her body, each kiss on her lips, on her skin, she tingled with remembrance and came close to moaning on the bus in which she sat. A flush crept up her face, and she bit her lips. But the erotic mood that had overtaken her didn't last long. The aftermath, the morning after, came crashing into her mind all too quickly.

By the time she'd awakened the next morning, he was gone. He'd sent a quick text on his way out: Have to catch that plane. Will call you.

She'd known of his pending trip to London and why he had to go; Duncan Tech had experienced some problems with their software out there, and they wanted Gabriel to help deal with the customer service fallout. His background in computer engineering would also help. She understood and sympathized with his reasons for slipping out during the night.

She texted him back as soon as she read his message. When he didn't respond, she thought perhaps he'd missed it or didn't find an opportunity to reply and had forgotten about it. Besides, she'd only sent a quick statement about their time together: Had a great time last night. Looking forward to seeing you when you return.

Sure, she'd hoped for a "me too" or something along those lines, but when she received nothing back, she justified his lack of response. It couldn't have been something she'd done. She'd felt and observed his desire for her. They'd had a wonderful time together. She wasn't the only one who'd enjoyed herself.

So, she texted a follow-up message: When will you be back?

He sent her an encouraging reply: Two months and we'll be back together.

Before the two months expired, Gabriel called her to say his father had fired the president and promoted Gabriel to the position. He suggested she move to London but didn't suggest they marry when she did, and Ellen considered that the beginning of the end. She couldn't leave her life, her family, for something so fragile and uncertain. She told him to resign and move back to Toronto. He refused. They split up. The next time she saw him, it was in the gossip rags and the entertainment news in the company of other women.

CHAPTER 4

Her day was already ruined, and it was still only 8:45 in the morning. Ellen barely made it to her desk with enough time to grab a coffee from the kitchen and organize for the meeting with Carol. Still a bit breathless, she carried a tablet with her to the meeting.

Carol's assistant told Ellen to go on in. "They're waiting for you."

They? She struggled to keep the surprise off her face and out of her voice as she said thank you to the assistant. Ellen rapped on the door before opening it and striding into the office. And almost collided with Gabriel Duncan, who stood near the door.

His expression flashed surprise rather than the shock and dismay that registered on Ellen's face. She instantly took a step back while he sidestepped to the chair he'd been sitting in.

"Ellen, it's you." His soothing baritone voice caressed her. "I didn't know you worked here."

Or you'd have gone somewhere else? Aloud, she said, "For almost three years now."

Carol, an athletic redhead who had landed the management position four years before, spoke in a cheerful voice, drawing Ellen's gaze in her direction. "You two know each other? Excellent. Then no need for introductions." She stood. "Ellen, Duncan Technologies has acquired a new company."

"I heard on the news." Ellen returned her gaze to Gabriel's face, focusing on his eyes. She refused to play shy. He had some nerve looking so delectable and together when the very sight of him wiped her brain of coherent thoughts. She'd have to rectify that right now. Anger replaced agony. In a steady voice, she said, "Congratulations. That's quite a coup."

"Thank you." He waited while she set her tablet on Carol's desk and settled into the chair beside him before taking his seat. They faced Carol, who sat at her desk once more, and let her take the controls.

"Ellen, obviously you're here because I want to assign you to take charge of BRI's financials. I know it's unusual to meet with the client in my office, but there are extenuating circumstances I want to discuss before you dig into their files. Before the buyout, BRI struggled to stay afloat. Expenses weren't keeping up with income, and in the few weeks before the buyout, they came close to declaring bankruptcy."

Turning to Gabriel, Ellen asked, "Then why buy them out? Aren't you just buying their problems?"

"I can turn them around," he replied smoothly. "When I did my due diligence, I discovered a lot of waste. They should've been doing well. It'll be easy to pull them out of the hole with the backing I have. Snapping them up now allowed me to get them at a bargain and saved the owners from personal bankruptcy. They appreciated the timing."

"Okay." She could accept that, but the company's financial downturn since she'd left continued to astound her. "But they were doing so well. What happened?"

"That's what you'll help me figure out. I want to identify every area of waste. They appeared to spend an awful lot of money on consultant fees for a shop that had a full contingent of programmers in-house. They never did that when you worked there. It's fortunate you're here." He paused, then said softly, "I didn't expect to find you here."

Captivated by the puzzle before her, Ellen pushed aside the million questions she wanted to ask him and contemplated everything he'd said before the pause. Finally, she spoke. "They never needed to hire overload workers from outside the company. They preferred to hire enough developers so they wouldn't have to contract out work. Finding experienced software developers is challenging. Getting them up to speed on your software and standards takes time in training. Did they get a sudden influx of projects that required extra hands?"

"Not that I could see." He shifted in his chair, angling his body toward her. "The extra expenses cropped up shortly after you left."

She frowned. "You think something's fishy with the books?"

"That's what you'll help me discover." He smiled, and her heart constricted.

She allowed the anger and bitterness of the last three years to quell her rising desire. "Of course, Mr. Duncan. I'll do everything I can to get to the bottom of it. Who's the current controller?"

His brows had risen at "Mr. Duncan," followed

immediately by a smirk he squelched so quickly she almost missed it. When he spoke, it wasn't to suggest she call him Gabriel—or Gabe, as she used to do. "I let her go. I got rid of extraneous staff as one way to save money."

When Ellen's face showed concern, he hurriedly said, "I gave her a more than fair severance package—well above what the law requires. She worked there less than three years, and I'm suspicious of the books. I couldn't keep her on. I need someone objective to review everything and clean up whatever needs cleaning up. The company should focus on development, not worry about accounting. That's your company's specialty. I prefer to turn that kind of thing over to experts."

She nodded. "I understand. When did you want to get started?"

"As soon as possible. I can have a login account set up for you today." He rose. "Thank you, Carol, for your time this morning. I'm sure I'll be more than pleased with the work your company does. If it's okay, I'll escort Miss Haddigan"—he squinted at Ellen as he said her name, and when he continued, he spoke directly to her—"to her desk so we can chat about the work she'll do."

Ellen ignored the formal use of her name. After all, she'd started it with that Mr. Duncan crack. She was willing to act civil if he was. With a glance at Carol, Ellen said, "I have a bit of time this morning." She stood.

Carol rose as well and held her hand out to Gabriel. As he clasped and shook it, she said, "That'll be fine. Ellen has other clients she's handling, but most of it is routine. She should be able to focus for the next while on your account. I'm sure she'll help you sort everything out." She smiled. "Ellen does excellent work. We're lucky to have her."

"Yes, I'm sure she'll do a great job."

Ellen examined his expression and tone for any sign of sarcasm and found none. She seethed.

Did I mean so little to him he doesn't care how I feel about what he did to me? Her hands curled into fists, and she had to control the urge to punch him in the gut.

She had to turn this account over to someone else. How could she work with him? But she didn't want to say anything in front of him. She'd go along with the assignment, remain professional and cool, and then talk to Carol about reassignment after he left.

Settled in her mind that this was the best course of action, Ellen picked up her tablet and calmly led him from Carol's office and down the hall to her cubicle.

CHAPTER 5

The shock of coming face to face with the woman who'd broken his heart almost made Gabriel lose his composure in Carol's office. Almost. He'd had three years to get over her, and he'd done a passable job of it. He'd even started dating again—had a date lined up for that evening, as a matter of fact. But the mere sight of Ellen Haddigan and her doe eyes and hair that looked so soft you wanted to run your fingers through it had him practically hyperventilating. But he played it cool the way she played it cool.

Her calm infuriated him. Of all the women in all the accounting companies in all of Toronto, she had to work at the one he'd hired to do his books. In a flash of practicality, he admitted having her manage the account was a stroke of luck. She was familiar with it and with how the business ran. Logic dictated he keep her on the project, especially since she seemed prepared to let bygones be bygones and keep things professional.

That reminder set his blood boiling again, but he

calmed himself with a few even breaths and won his way through the meeting in Carol's office. He expected the private meeting with Ellen would tax his nerves, but when they stepped through the doorway into the room where she had her desk, he was relieved to see she had a cubicle among two rows of three cubicles each. They wouldn't be alone. They'd have no chance to get personal. He'd only have to remain detached, stay smooth, and he'd breeze through the discussion unscathed.

She ushered him to a chair and took a seat next to him in front of her computer. The machine was already booted up, which spared him the small talk that typically went with waiting for technology to prep itself. She went immediately to the BRI company website and asked him for access.

He focused his attention on business. If she wanted to play it that way, he'd go along with it, but there'd come a point when they'd have to discuss their history. He'd started falling in love with her, for God's sake. She owed him the consideration of an explanation for why she not only refused to move to London but also cut off all contact with him.

He'd always told himself he hadn't loved her. Not yet. Not then. He'd only *started* to fall for her and had gotten out just in time. Thank God he hadn't done something stupid like telling her he loved her.

The more his thoughts roamed to the past, the more infuriated he grew until he could barely keep the rage from his voice. His face must've betrayed something of what he felt because Ellen stopped talking in the middle of a sentence he hadn't even heard. A startled expression crossed her face, and she licked her lips and wrung her hands in a display of nerves he'd not seen from her today.

"What is it?" she asked.

Wrong way to open the conversation. Gabriel scowled. When he spoke, he kept his voice low and discreet, but even he heard the menace in his tone. "What could possibly be wrong? Miss Haddigan. That's correct, isn't it? Miss?"

She swallowed, her throat bobbing and giving a little click as she did. "Yes. I mean, you can call me Ellen. We're working together." She glanced away as she said that last bit, and it aroused his suspicions.

"That's not what I mean," he snapped, still keeping his voice low. "You didn't marry?" He glanced at her left hand. No engagement ring, never mind a wedding ring. If life were fair, her fiancé had dumped her, and she'd suffered as much as Gabriel had when he'd heard she was engaged.

"Marry?" The shock that crossed her face and the surprise in her voice confused him.

"Yes, marry. Did you think I'd never find out you were engaged? What happened to lover boy?"

She remained silent for a long while, and he let her stew in whatever juices traitors like her stewed. When she finally spoke again, her words, had he not been sitting, would've knocked him on his ass.

"I don't know what you're talking about. I've never been engaged. The closest I came to having a boyfriend in the last three years was—" She snapped her mouth closed, but when he opened his, she cut him off, saying, "You must have me confused with another woman you seduced and abandoned."

"Seduced." He leaned forward in his chair, his eyes narrowing. "To my recollection, you didn't need much seducing. You were all over me like ticks on a deer."

31

"What the hell is wrong with you?" Her voice had risen, and he heard shuffling in the surrounding cubicles. If she didn't keep it down, they'd be the talk of the office—if they weren't already.

She leaned back in her chair, sorrow marring her features and breaking his heart all over again. "This won't work, Gabe. We can't work together. I'll ask Carol to reassign me."

The use of his nickname made his breath catch.

"That might be best." He'd still be forced to run into her in the halls. Maybe he could arrange to meet with her replacement outside the office. But he had one more item to address before they parted ways. She'd seemed genuinely puzzled when he'd asked about the engagement, yet his source for the information had been a trusted one.

"You didn't get engaged after you left BRI?"

"Oh, Gabe, where the hell would you get that idea?" She propped her elbows on her desk and dropped her head in her palms.

Neither one spoke for a few moments, and he mulled over the implications of the conversation. Had he wasted the last whole year he'd been back in Toronto refusing to track her down? Was it all his fault? If everything he'd believed was wrong, then yes, it was all his fault, and he was a jerk.

"I heard ..." He couldn't continue. What exactly had happened then? How had things gone from a wild, passionate night that harbingered the start of a solid relationship to cold heartache within six months?

"You heard what? From whom?" She averted her gaze and surreptitiously swiped at her eyes with one hand.

Great. He'd brought her to tears.

"It's not important right now." He didn't want to tell her until he'd verified it himself. Was it possible he'd gotten it all wrong? It couldn't be. He'd heard it from someone who'd known Ellen at BRI.

"Is that why you dated every nubile young thing in England?"

"What? No. I mean, I didn't date."

"Really." Her tone dripped contempt. "I've kept the articles. The pictures." As soon as the words were out, she flushed so red she glowed.

He huffed out an exasperated breath, and he shook his head. "Are you telling me," he said, enunciating each word, "that you got your information about my personal life from gossip rags?" And if what she'd said was true, she'd not only read them but also kept the articles. The pictures.

"I …" She put her head in her palms again. When she looked up, her eyes were damp. "We both made stupid assumptions. If you thought I was engaged, why didn't you contact me and ask me about it?"

Irritation surged up again, overriding regret and sorrow. "Contact you? After you dumped me?"

"If that's what you think, I won't press it, but obviously, we shouldn't work together. Why don't you leave for now, and I'll have a talk with Carol—explain the situation? She'll understand." Ellen sounded dubious as she said that, but he let it go.

But she was right. Seeing her, hearing her voice on the phone, being near her and unable to touch her or, quite frankly, have sex with her would torture him.

"All right." He stood, and she rose at the same time. "You look good, Ellen." She really did. It took all his self-control to keep his hands off her. It'd been so long since they'd last kissed, but he still remembered how she tasted.

"Thank you. You too."

"For what it's worth, I'm sorry," he said. "For everything. I made an error in judgment." Something he'd rectify as soon as he left this office. Someone he trusted had steered him wrong, and he intended to find out why. But first, he needed to salvage something of the relationship with Ellen. The fury and heartache he'd experienced since he'd heard she was engaged melted away to be replaced with a panic that he'd possibly let the most promising relationship of his life slip away.

"We need to talk about this but not here," he said.

"No, we really don't." She shook her head for emphasis, but her eyes were sad and her expression regretful.

"You probably think I don't deserve it, and you're probably correct, but give me a chance." Should he remind her of how hot and sexy that one night had been and how well they'd meshed in the months before that night? He almost spoke up but then feared it would lead to a long discussion at the office within earshot of her coworkers. Worse yet, what if it led to an argument? He could damage her reputation and humiliate her in front of her coworkers, if he hadn't already done so. The office around them had fallen pin-drop silent, only the occasional mouse click or keyboard tapping evident.

Ellen apparently drew the same conclusion, because she rose from her seat to peer over the cubicle and scope out the area. Relief washed across her face, and she sat down again. "All right. I don't want to talk here, so I'll meet you tonight after work." She suggested they meet at the saloon at five. "But I'll still ask Carol to remove me from your account."

"Would you be willing to wait until after we talk?" He gave her a pleading look.

The smile she gave him was inadvertent and genuine, and it eased a knot in his gut he hadn't noticed was there until it disappeared.

"Stop looking at me like that. You know—" She cut herself off, but she'd wanted to say "You know I can't resist that look." He knew it as well as he knew her—or the her he'd known and fallen for—*not loved, I didn't love her*—over three years ago. He'd used the look on her often enough under more congenial circumstances.

"I think you should leave now." She said it in a low voice, not angry or emotional, just a little tired.

He knew when to toss in his cards and go home with the pot. Gabriel rose.

"I'll see you at five. Foundation Saloon, yeah?" He scanned the room as he spoke, verifying no one was peeking over the cubicle walls. He didn't care what they thought of him, but if he could spare Ellen embarrassment, he'd inconvenience himself to do it.

"Yes, I'll be there," she replied.

He left the office, the knot in his gut increasing with every step away from her he took.

CHAPTER 6

It wasn't until Gabriel reached his car in the basement parking lot that he remembered he had a date that evening. No problem—he'd make sure he didn't stay long with Ellen. He wasn't about to cancel a date with a woman who attracted him when his relationship with Ellen had ended under such catastrophic and dramatic circumstances. First things first, though. He sat in his BMW with the engine off and called Carl, the close friend and business associate who'd told him Ellen was engaged.

"Carl Walker."

"I got a question for you, pal." Gabriel had difficulty keeping his tone casual.

"Gabe? What's up?"

"Who told you Ellen was engaged?"

"A woman she'd worked with. When I asked her where Ellen went after she left BRI, the woman said Ellen got engaged about six months after she left the company. I didn't get any details—she said she didn't know anything."

"Who was the woman?"

"One of the software developers. A blonde."

"That doesn't narrow it down. Which blonde?"

"How many blonde female developers worked there? Dude, I dealt with the marketing department."

Gabriel exhaled loudly into the phone. "I talked to Ellen today, and she knew nothing about this." The anger leaked out now. "She claims she never was engaged. Didn't even have a boyfriend, let alone a fiancé."

"Are you serious? You mean you never talked to her before now?"

"I believed you. And we'd broken up." Except that it wasn't simply trust in Carl that had kept him from calling her, was it? If pressed, he'd have to admit his ego had suffered. She'd left BRI within a month of their breakup. An engagement implied she'd already had something going on the side. The reminder stirred his fury again despite the knowledge the rumour was false.

"Yeah, but to not talk to her?"

"What would've been the point?" Except if he had, she'd have straightened him out, and he wouldn't have wasted the last year without her. Gabriel pounded a fist on the steering wheel. "Christ, Carl, I cut her out of my life. I assumed she was over me, that I hadn't meant much to her."

"You know what they say about that, eh? When you assume? U, me, ass."

"That's not funny."

"No, but it's true. You'll have to learn not to assume the worst about people. It's burned you before. I thought you'd at least talk to her, even if all you did was find out who the guy was and congratulate her."

"I couldn't. I didn't want to ruin her life by showing up after all this time." The lie made him squirm where he sat, but he couldn't admit to his friend how devastated the news had made him. He hoped the decision to not call her wouldn't cost him his happiness forever. It'd already cost him this last year.

He ended the call with Carl, trying not to hold him responsible for what had happened. He started the car but didn't put it into gear. Instead, he turned his thoughts back to that night—that wonderful, awful night with Ellen.

The moment she'd invited him back to her apartment, he knew she wanted him as much as he wanted her. All those months of flirting and uncertainty had culminated in this, and he couldn't have been happier. He never pushed her into anything—he made sure of that—and they hadn't had too much to drink before and during the meal they'd shared. He'd sensed this would be the night they became intimate, and he didn't want alcohol to cloud her judgment. So, when she'd made clear to him she was not only willing but also eager to take him to her bed, he knew she meant it.

Recalling what they'd done together as soon as they stepped into her apartment still aroused him. He'd relived it in the sleepless nights he'd had since then, but these remembrances always ended in pain and fury. They'd both known he'd leave for London the next day, and that they'd have to have a long-distance relationship, but they'd expected his absence to last only two months.

Two weeks into his trip, though, his father appeared in Gabriel's temporary office, and that changed everything. His father made an excellent case for why

Gabriel should remain in London. The experience the promotion would give him would prepare him to take over the entire company when his father retired. Losing the president had left that branch in dire straits, and his father insisted their best strategy was for Gabriel to take the post. While it wasn't what he'd wanted to do with his life, he couldn't say no to his dad. He had to stay on, and he wanted Ellen to join him.

Admittedly, he'd broached the subject inappropriately. He assumed she loved him and would be eager to pick up stakes and move to London to be with him. So what if it wasn't a proposal of marriage? Didn't they need to do a test-run first to see if it was the real thing?

As they argued about it over the airwaves and the ocean between them, Gabriel came close to saying the words that might've changed everything. Not "marry me" but "I love you." However, the words never left his lips—nor hers, if it came to it, so his behaviour was justified—and before he knew what had happened, he found himself sitting on the side of his hotel room bed with a silent phone in his hand. They'd never spoken again. Until now.

As soon as he'd laid eyes on her this morning in Carol's office, all his feelings for her returned in force as if no time at all had passed.

Gabriel drove from the parking lot and headed to his new company, ready to focus on work for a while.

***

Confusion and tension greeted Gabriel when he stepped into the BRI office building. People scurried through the hallways as though scrambling to important meetings, their expressions strained. Gabriel strode through the lobby to the reception desk and found himself second in line to a police detective who introduced himself to the receptionist as Detective Howard Morris. He followed that up with what sounded like a request, but Gabriel didn't catch the words.

Morris wore a parka, though it hung open revealing a black suit, so Gabriel assumed the man had arrived recently. The receptionist, a prim woman in a tailored navy dress whose name Gabriel couldn't recall even though it'd been only a week ago he'd visited, greeted him and returned to her conversation with the detective. She introduced herself to the man as Karen, jogging Gabriel's memory.

She offered to take Morris's coat, and he shrugged out of it and passed it to her. Gabriel had left his coat in his car, which was parked in the building's underground lot.

"What's going on here?" Gabriel asked.

"Detective Morris asked to speak to the owner of the company. I was just trying to figure out whether I should call your office or your cell." She turned from Gabriel to the detective. "Mr. Duncan bought BRI and assumed control three weeks ago." She looked hesitantly at Gabriel and then directed her words to him. "Your assistant said you'd be in today."

"Where is Mr. Merrick?" the detective asked, referring to BRI's former owner.

"At home. He's been in and out these last few weeks, helping with the transition, but as of this morning, he won't be coming in anymore. Do you want his phone number?"

"I have his contact information already. I wanted to

start with the BRI offices. I assumed he'd be here today."

As the conversation paused, Gabriel cut in. "Start what, Detective?"

Morris glanced at Karen and said, "May we speak privately, Mr. Duncan?"

"Sure. Is the conference room available, Karen?"

She checked her computer and replied, "Conference Room A is free. It's unlocked."

"Thank you. Can you ask someone to bring us coffee, please?" When she said she'd take care of it, Gabriel led the detective to the elevators. As they walked, he asked, "What's this about?"

"Do you know Francesca Newton?"

"We've never met, but I know she worked here as a controller. I let her go three weeks ago." He chose not to elaborate with anything else until the detective revealed why he asked.

They arrived on the third floor and walked the short distance to Conference Room A. Morris stepped in ahead of Gabriel when he opened the door. He shivered in the room's empty chill and switched on the gas fireplace behind the eight-seat conference table.

Though sparsely furnished, the room was small and would heat quickly. The wallpaper looked slightly out of date, as did the painting on the wall. A low cabinet underneath the painting held a glass vase with flowers offset to the right of the painting. Gabriel made a mental note to have the entire floor of offices and rooms that belonged to them redecorated.

"Have a seat, Detective." Gabriel took a seat at the end of the mahogany table.

Morris sat on Gabriel's left in the padded chair and produced a notebook and pen from his suit jacket.

When they were both settled, Gabriel asked, "What's this about, then?"

"I'm afraid I have some bad news."

"Did something happen to Miss Newton?" Gabriel tried to remember if he'd heard anything from or about Francesca Newton after telling Bradley to give her a severance package. Perhaps she was suing the company for wrongful termination. But that wouldn't require a detective.

"Yes. She was found deceased last night, and the death is suspicious."

CHAPTER 7

At five o'clock, Ellen walked into the Foundation Saloon and, when she gave her name, the hostess led her to a table with a booth near the back of the dining room. Gabriel was already there, a half-empty stein of beer in front of him.

"Got an early start?" she asked. The hostess set a menu in front of Ellen, who took a seat across from him.

He waited for the hostess to leave and then said, his expression serious, his tone dark, "We have a problem."

She smiled—a cross between a smirk and amusement. "You being dramatic?"

"No. You ever hear of Francesca Newton?"

"I trained her on the financial software BRI uses. She replaced me as controller when I quit."

He leaned toward her and said in a low voice, "She's dead."

Cold dread washed over Ellen. "What do you mean dead?"

43

"When I got to the BRI offices today, a detective was there. He told me her husband found her body in their apartment. Looks like suicide, but the police are investigating and treating it as a suspicious death."

"I'm sorry to hear that. She seemed like a nice woman. Young. What a waste. I'm sure it's just a routine investigation. They do that for any death that isn't natural, don't they?" And why would this be a problem for her, or more specifically, them? There was no "them."

"He said there were indications she was murdered."

The oxygen in the room seemed to vanish and Ellen gasped. "What indications?"

"He wouldn't tell me. But if they think someone killed her, they likely have evidence."

She nodded, unable to speak.

Francesca had been a pretty woman in her late twenties. She'd been so full of life. Yes, that was a cliché, but in Francesca's case, it was an accurate description. The young woman had been eager to start the new job and learned the software quickly. Ellen had been positive she'd work out well.

"What could've happened?" she said aloud though she spoke more to herself than to Gabriel.

He replied anyway. "I don't know."

She recalled his comment at the start of the conversation. "Why is this a problem for us?" The publicity might be bad for him, but she'd left that company too long ago for anyone to associate her with it. Unless she took over their books, as Carol had assigned her to do.

She needed to clear this up immediately. "It won't be a problem for me. I'm not taking the account. Are you really thinking only of the bad press over this? A woman died. She either killed herself or someone murdered her. Isn't that more important than what the media might say about you over it?"

Anger flared in his eyes and he scowled. "That's not where my mind went. How could you think that?"

"Why wouldn't I think that? I don't know you anymore. What else is there?"

"Don't you think it's strange that such a successful company went downhill after you left?"

Before she could respond, the server, a perky, petite redhead with braids and freckles, arrived to take Ellen's drink order. Deciding she needed one, she ordered a glass of red wine—the nine-ounce rather than the six-ounce option. When the woman left, Ellen picked up the menu. She didn't feel hungry, but stress eating was one of her go-to coping mechanisms, and the news of what could be the murder of an acquaintance had definitely stressed her.

"Want to order food?" she asked.

When he remained silent, she peeked up from the menu. He stared at her, his lips pressed together.

"What's wrong?" Did he think her callous for wanting to order food? "I stress eat, Gabe. I'm not heartless."

He set his palms on the table, bracketing his mug of beer, and said, "It's not that. I have to leave soon. I'm going somewhere else for dinner."

Her whole body went cold. "You have a date," she stated. "On a Thursday."

"Yes. One I made two weeks ago. I'm sort of seeing someone ..."

"Sort of?" Francesca's death popped into her head, and she waved a hand at him. "Never mind. I don't care. You're free to see whomever you want and do whatever you want with her. What matters is what happened to Fran."

He gave her a slow nod. "Right. So, answer my question."

"What question?"

"The company was prosperous. They had substantial revenues. Still do, from what I can tell. Their problems started after you left."

She gasped. "You pinning that on Fran? Is that why you think she killed herself?"

"Or was murdered."

Ellen brushed a hand through her hair, pulling errant strands off her face. The server arrived with her wine and set it in front of her.

"I'll take an order of sweet potato fries," Ellen told her. "Nothing for him," she added with a nod in Gabriel's direction.

After the redhead left again, Gabriel checked the time on his phone. "I have to go. Drinks and your food are on me. I'll settle the tab on my way out. Order anything else you want. They'll put it on my card." He gazed at her contemplatively for a moment. "Don't use it to get revenge on me."

"Wow. Don't worry. I can pay for my own food."

"That was a joke, Ellen. Can we please forget the past? I'm sorry for what happened. We'll figure it out. In the meantime, help me with BRI. Take on the account. Maybe, together, we can figure out if anything in the records could've triggered her death, whether by her own hand or someone else's."

"I don't know. What I'll do is think about it tonight and give you an answer in the morning. If I decide we shouldn't work together, I'll tell Carol to give it to someone else."

"But you know the company already. If anyone can spot inconsistencies or anything that's not right, you can."

"You think she was deliberately cooking the books?"

"How would I know? It could be anything. You'd find the issue faster than anyone else. Will you do it?"

She pictured herself working with Gabriel, perhaps for weeks. She'd see or talk to him every day, given the unusual situation. But he was correct she'd find errors faster than anyone else. Plus, if it helped the police catch a killer or helped them understand why Francesca killed herself, didn't Ellen owe it to everyone to do anything she could to figure it out?

Reluctantly, she said, "On one condition: When I've post-mortemed the files, when I've cleaned them up and everything's in order, you turn the account over to someone else."

"No problem," he blurted. His expression told her he thought by that point she'd change her mind.

Ellen swore to herself she wouldn't. She'd give him no choice but to put someone else on the account. By the time this was over, she'd find another job and remove herself from Gabriel's life the way he'd removed himself from hers three years ago.

She reached out her hand. "Deal."

They shook on it, and he walked away, her gaze following him out of sight.

CHAPTER 8

Even though she didn't enjoy eating alone, she ordered a plate of wings to go with the fries as soon as she lost sight of Gabriel. If he was paying for it, she might as well. While she was at it, she ordered another glass of wine—a more expensive one this time. Her own credit cards were close to maxed out, and her most recent online shopping spree didn't help. Once more, she vowed to reduce her spending, but how the hell could she do that when Gabriel's presence added more stress to her life and she stress shopped as often as she stress ate?

While she waited for her food and wine to arrive, she contemplated what she knew about Francesca. Would the detective want to talk to Ellen about the death even though she hadn't worked with the victim in almost three years? Even then, it was only for about two weeks—long enough to show Francesca how things worked and then leave.

After she'd left BRI, Ellen had fallen into a depression that lasted for six weeks. She didn't search for new employment, and she did a lot of shopping and eating. She ran her credit cards up and gained ten pounds. By the time it was all over, she'd given up her apartment and moved back in with her parents to get her life back in order.

While it would be easy to lay the blame for her breakdown at Gabriel's feet, she had to admit he could only take a small portion of accountability for it. Most of the fault lay with her. She'd given him her heart, had trusted him, and he'd betrayed her. He'd returned to Toronto and hadn't contacted her. What was worse, he'd believed a rumour and hadn't had the decency to confront her. What did it say about him that he'd give up on her so easily? What did it say about her that she wasn't worth pursuing?

This proved they shouldn't be together. All she had to do was clean up his books and move on to something else. Another company. Or she'd start her own business and accept only the jobs she wanted.

A man's voice interrupted her plotting. "Hi. You by yourself tonight?"

When she looked up, she found John Aylmer, the man she'd met when she'd celebrated her birthday here with Rhonda, staring back at her.

"Hi. Yup. Just me tonight."

"Feel like company?"

He hadn't lit a fire in her the way Gabriel instantly had when they'd first met, but he was nice enough. She indicated the empty bench across from her and said, "Have a seat. Help yourself to the fries. I've got wings coming too."

John waved the server over and sat. After ordering a beer, he plucked a fry off her plate and ate it.

"Where's Max tonight?" she asked.

49

"Out. With your friend." He didn't sound annoyed by the turn of events.

"So you came here by yourself?"

"No. I had a blind date. We were meeting here." He chuckled a little. "She cancelled the moment I arrived." He waved a hand at her. "I was still in the parking lot, so she didn't see me. I'm sure it was legit. I figured I'd come in and eat anyway, seeing how I was already here. Spotted you when I walked in and thought we could commiserate."

"Rhonda never told me she was seeing Max tonight." Ellen checked her phone and saw two missed text messages. She checked them and both were from Rhonda. The first said she was going out with Max that evening and the second provided restaurant details.

"I guess she did tell me." She'd been too absorbed with Gabriel to notice. *No, I was too gobsmacked by news of Francesca's possible murder.*

She quickly responded to Rhonda's texts: Have a great time and let me know when you're home.

Their drinks arrived then, followed shortly after by the chicken wings.

"So," he asked, "how's the accounting business treating you?"

"Fine. Busy. It's always busy." She didn't want to talk about her work and especially didn't want to say anything about Francesca and BRI. "How's the labour law game?"

He smiled. "Fine. Busy. It's always busy."

"Lots of lawsuits?"

"I don't know what constitutes a lot. More now, I guess, since the economy took a downturn. That's expected though." He leaned back on the bench, draping one arm casually across the back. "I guess

50

you're getting more business these days as well?"

"They've assigned me more accounts lately. Not sure if it's related to the economy or if my coworkers are also getting more assignments. Some companies see a savings by farming the financial accounting out to another company rather than hiring employees." She really didn't want to talk about work. Time to change the subject. "So, what did Max say to you about Rhonda?"

"You want me to rat him out to you so you can report to her? I don't think so."

"Okay, what do you think of Rhonda? Are they compatible?"

"I'm not getting involved in this discussion."

"Geez, what a lawyer. She's a great woman. He'd be lucky to have her."

John waggled his brows, making Ellen laugh.

"That's not how I meant it." She relaxed in her seat and sipped her wine. "Fine. Tell me what you do in your spare time when you're not lawyering and evading questions about your friend Max."

Since Ellen no longer obsessed over the past—she had the present to obsess over now—she allowed herself to relax and enjoy the distraction John's company provided. He proved to be pleasant and an intelligent conversationalist. They had little in common—he preferred sports to anything else, and she preferred anything else to sports—but the evening passed swiftly enough. When she next glanced at the time on her cell phone, it was almost ten.

"I gotta go," she said. "Don't worry about the two beers you had. They're covered."

His brows raised. "Your company picking up this tab?"

"In a way." She smiled. "I'll see you around." She rose.

"Wait. Can I see you again?"

"Sure. Come say hello when our paths cross."

He paused, frowned. "I enjoyed your company. I thought maybe we could do this again sometime."

She slid back into her seat. "I had fun, too, John, but I'm not looking for a relationship."

"Me neither. Just casual. Not a date."

"I hate sports. What would we do?"

"You like to eat. We could get together for a dinner now and then. Drinks. Conversation. Like tonight. You know, since Max and Rhonda will probably spend more time together, you and I will need to find something to do."

She laughed. "I've got an idea: My parents are having a cocktail party on Saturday. My mother's trying to play matchmaker, and she's invited friends who have sons—and the sons too. I'll put you, Rhonda, and Max on the guest list. You can be my pretend date. That'll fend off the potential suitors. It'll be perfect."

He grinned. "I've always wanted to be a fake boyfriend."

"Oh, they won't buy that. You'll have to be a fake potential boyfriend."

"I can live with that." He held up his phone. "Give me the details. I'll let Max know we've got plans Saturday night. Then you can spy on them and decide for yourself if he's good enough for her."

She faked indignation. "That never once entered my mind." But it had, and she planned to make sure Rhonda wasn't setting herself up for heartache. If she could prevent Max from hurting Rhonda the way Gabriel had hurt Ellen, she'd do it.

CHAPTER 9

On Friday, Ellen dove into the files Gabriel provided her access to after she did some housekeeping for her other clients. She'd spend most of the day reviewing the account in the system on BRI's server.

Since she could work at her desk and access their books remotely, she'd avoid seeing Gabriel and focus on the work—a bonus as far as she was concerned. This all allowed her to get reacquainted with the workings of BRI's business and get an impression of the work Francesca had done.

Already, she suspected something wasn't right. Certain entries stood out most to her. The company hired temp workers and contractors far too often for the amount of work they had, and their expenses had increased by too much from previous years.

It hadn't started immediately. Ellen calculated Francesca worked at BRI about six months before the expenses jumped and profits dropped. Billings had increased as well, but Ellen noticed places where the payments didn't match what the developer originally had billed in hours to BRI's clients. It would take her a few weeks to really dig into what had happened, and she'd need to interview various employees of the company. She should discuss this with Gabriel.

As she reached for the office phone on her desk, she hesitated. Did she really need to review this with him, or was she calling just to hear his voice? Or, worse yet, find out how his date last night went? If this were any other client, would she make the call?

Frustrated that she second-guessed her motives, she picked up the phone and, before she could change her mind, called him. His assistant put her through, and he picked up on the first ring.

"Gabriel Duncan."

"It's Ellen."

"Hey, Ellen, what can I do for you?" He sounded happy. It pissed her off.

"I've found some inconsistencies. It might help if I could work at your offices next week, interview some of the staff still around. How many did you let go?"

"Everyone from accounting ... three there ... none of the software developers ... human resources ... that's another two—I consolidated the roles and replaced them with my own person."

"No one else?"

"I don't want the expense of full-time employees for accounting. Far more efficient to farm that out. We develop software. That's where I want to focus. HR because they didn't have a handle on the contractors they supposedly hired, and with accounting gone, we wouldn't need more than one person."

"I thought you want to expand the company?"

"Yes, with business, not employees."

"Who was the HR manager? Was it still Moira

Wilson?"

"Yes."

Ellen fell silent, and Gabriel allowed it to stretch while she contemplated what he'd told her. Finally, she said, "I'd have trusted Moira. She worked there for five years before I left."

"Still, I had someone else in mind for that position. I've worked with him before and trust him."

"Moira wouldn't have done anything wrong."

"I'm not saying she did. I'm setting up the team I want working for me."

"All right. I'll buy that. How did she take it when you let her go?"

"Moira? She understood. I made sure she received a decent package, made sure they all did. More than fair. I enquired about her today. She's already found another job."

"So, everyone else at BRI is still the same?"

"Don't know if anyone you know quit or was let go before I bought the place. They weren't a revolving door, but you left, and you're not the only one to do so in the last three years."

"Sure. People move on." Which was a lie. Had she really moved on, or had she just come full circle? Before she could stop herself, she said, "How was your date last night?"

"Great segue. Not that it's any of your business, but we had a good time."

"How good?" Oh, God, did that really come out of her mouth?

He laughed in surprise. "That's a bold question. The date was fine."

She'd already crossed the line so nothing else she said could make things worse. Ellen pressed on.

"Anyone I might know?"

"Katrina."

Ellen sucked in a breath as the blood rushed from her face. "Not Katrina Weever?"

"As a matter of fact, yes. Why?"

"Nothing. Well, yes, something. She worked at BRI when I was there."

"She doesn't anymore, so if you're worried about a conflict, there isn't one. She's a programmer at an insurance firm now. One of the ones who, as you said, moved on."

The silence dragged on, Ellen refusing to break it.

"You jealous?"

"Not at all." But she was. "You officially dating after last night?"

"Where's this going, Ellen?"

"Just making small talk. Glad your date went well. I'll come over to BRI first thing Monday morning and work from there. Okay?"

"Yeah."

"Great, see you then." She went to disconnect but heard him call out her name. She pressed the phone back to her ear. "Yes?"

"If you must know, I didn't set up another date with her."

"You didn't have to tell me that." Relief flooded through her.

"See you Monday." He ended the call.

***

Saturday dawned sunny but cold. Snow blanketed the ground. By the time Ellen and her mother arrived at the spa, the temperature had risen to above zero and the snow on the sidewalks had turned to a soft grey slush. Ellen had informed her mother they'd have an extra three guests that night, and Joanne reacted with a mix of annoyance and curiosity. Certain her mother would confront her on it as they sat in the steam room, Ellen braced for impact the moment their towels were settled under their bare behinds.

Sure enough, Joanne opened with a comment about the new beau—a word that made Ellen giggle involuntarily.

"He's not my beau. I only met him recently. We're not at the beau stage yet. He's yet to earn that status." She giggled again.

"Are you mocking me?"

Ellen put a hand on her mother's shoulder. "Never. I find the word 'beau' archaic. It sounds funny." She dropped her hand, resting it on her thigh.

"I hoped you'd hit it off with one of my friend's sons."

"Don't worry about me. I can take care of myself." Which was obviously a lie since she depended on her parents for shelter. Ellen determined to change that. She'd wallowed long enough, and with Gabriel back in the country, she could resolve the past and move forward. Perhaps John would become more than just a fake boyfriend, and she'd start seeing him for real. Too bad the chemistry wasn't there, and they had next to nothing in common.

"I know. You did so well before, and you'll recover. Dad and I will always be here for you if you need us, but you're more than capable of success on your own. You'd be happier, though, with a husband, children. I know you. You don't like to be alone."

"I don't especially like to be around people." Which

also wasn't true. She sought out the company of others, loved to attend concerts and events with large crowds. They energized her, helped her recharge. So why did she deny this to her mother?

"Okay," she admitted, "I like being around people, but I don't have to have a husband or children—especially children." She wrinkled her nose in distaste. "They're a lot of work and messy and needy. Yuck."

"But look at Laura," Joanne said, referring to Ellen's older sister. "She's been married five years now and has one child and another on the way."

"She loves it. I don't. Not everyone is cut out to raise kids."

"Don't worry." Now Joanne placed a reassuring hand on Ellen's shoulder. "You'll find someone and settle down to have a family."

"Sure," Ellen replied and exhaled a sigh. *Did she even hear a word I said?*

CHAPTER 10

After Ellen and her mother finished at the spa, they went for lunch and then to the hair salon to have their hair done. While she was there, Ellen picked up some beauty supplies, promising herself this was the last time she sprang for expensive hair care products and makeup until the credit card balances dropped. When they returned to the house, Ellen's father greeted them at the door.

"So, how did my ladies enjoy their day?" Alan Haddigan asked.

"Great," Joanne replied. "We had a lovely time. How do you like Ellen's hair?"

He appraised her trimmed, straightened hair. "You look gorgeous, dear."

"Thanks, Dad. How was your trip?" she replied.

Her father had returned from a business trip to Montreal the day before. He worked as a director of sales for a dairy company and travelled all over the world visiting sales teams at their various offices.

A lean, handsome man, you couldn't tell by looking

at him that in five years he'd retire. His dark hair had only touches of grey at the temples, and his olive skin resisted wrinkles much better than Joanne's pale face and dry skin.

Ellen and her mother looked forward to his retirement day with anticipation and more than a little trepidation. They wanted him to relax and enjoy leisure time, but he loved to work. The women both hoped he'd adjust to the retiree life, but they weren't sure he would.

"The trip went well. Helped secure a few contracts we didn't have before. All ready for tonight?"

Ellen told them she had a few things to do and would come upstairs for the party, and she rushed to her basement bedroom to change her clothes. She searched through her closet for something suitable, which meant something attractive but not alluring. She didn't want to give John the impression she desired anything intimate from their relationship. As she settled on a simple navy sheath dress, her cell phone sounded, and she scurried to dig it from her purse. She noted Rhonda's name and number on the call display and accepted the call.

"Hi, Rhonda, how was your date last night?"

As ordered, Rhonda had texted Ellen after the date, but the two hadn't spoken since.

"Wonderful." Her voice dropped to a whisper. "He's still here." She giggled, an uncharacteristic sound coming from her, and said, "He's making brunch for us in my kitchen as we speak."

Ellen glanced at the time. "Brunch? You're getting dangerously close to linner. Don't tell me you're just getting out of bed."

"What the hell's linner?" Rhonda asked.

Ellen laughed. "Well, brunch is breakfast and lunch. Linner is—"

"Lunch and dinner. Gotcha." Rhonda giggled again. "Guilty. Oh, Ellen, he's so great. I think he might be 'the one.'"

Chills ran up Ellen's spine, but she tried to control her fear. She didn't want to begrudge Rhonda her happiness, but, based on her own experience, her friend could wind up getting seriously hurt.

Reservation in her voice, Ellen said, "That's wonderful. Shouldn't you be helping him?"

What if he was drugging her eggs? Her coffee? Ellen shook off the insane thoughts as Rhonda chattered on about the wonderful dinner they'd had, the romantic stroll they'd taken along Lake Ontario's shores, and tidbits about the night they spent in bed. Apparently, Max was an overachiever in the sack as well as in the courtroom.

"I'm so happy for you." Again, her words belied her true feelings.

"I can hear it in your voice, Ellen. What's wrong?"

"Not a thing!" she replied, injecting confidence and assurance into her tone. "Sounds like you're perfect for each other. I'm just gun-shy."

"Not all men are Gabriel Duncan. Remind yourself of that whenever you're tempted to trounce another man. Max won't hurt me. He's incapable of it. Besides, he's told me already he wants a serious relationship. A wife. Kids."

"You're joking." Again, her radar went on high alert. "Isn't that a bit fast?"

"Fast if you're a teenager. When you're our age," she said, making it sound as if the early thirties conferred wisdom on them previous years hadn't, "you know what you want. You don't have to experiment to see what you like. It's so much nicer this way."

"I didn't know you had a firm criteria list." Sure, they'd discussed what they'd want in a man, but Ellen never expected either of them to find it. Ellen's Mister Perfect resembled Aragorn from the *Lord of the Rings*. What would a shrink make of that? Was he too perfect? Too regal and wise? Too hot?

"I've always had a list. I've adapted it over the years. Max ticks every box. He just doesn't have the blond hair."

Ellen laughed. "You wanted a blond? Why didn't you sit next to John when you had the chance? You got to the table first."

"I don't know. Something about how they greeted me. John scowled a little—as if he preferred I sit next to Max. And he stared at you as if he couldn't take his eyes off you."

"Curious. We didn't have chemistry, and I wasn't drawn to him at all. He's good-looking, and objectively, he's a catch—you know, a good-on-paper guy—but I'm not interested."

"My dear, you still have it bad for Gabriel, and if you don't erase him from your psyche, you'll never be happy."

"You're right. Maybe tonight I'll do that."

***

By 7:30 that evening, the Haddigan home was filled with guests. Ellen wove her way through the throng in the living room and arrived in the kitchen, which was also crowded with people. She smiled and chatted as she meandered her way to the buffet counter where the bottles of alcohol were set up. She refilled her wineglass with a robust Shiraz from Australia and sipped it before turning back to head into the dining room where the snacks were laid out on the dining room table.

Rhonda, Max, and John had arrived exactly at seven, and Joanne and Alan greeted them with enthusiasm. They'd paid particular attention to John, and Ellen had made her escape to the kitchen so she wouldn't have to listen to the interrogation.

She made small talk with her parents' friends, who introduced her to their eligible sons, none of whom made her insides churn the way Gabriel did. Used to. Okay, still did. Would she ever get over him?

As if sensing her thoughts on him, her cell phone sounded with Gabriel's ringtone: Alanis Morrisette's "You Oughta Know." She fumbled with the phone, trying to answer it before someone recognized the song.

This is what happens when you drunk-select a ringtone. She'd set it after she'd returned home the night she had drinks with John while Gabriel was probably still on his date with Katrina. Ellen forced herself to say Katrina's name every time she thought about Gabriel and his date. It helped keep the fires of fury lit.

Pressing the phone to her ear, she said, "Yeah?" She hadn't meant to be abrupt, but that's how it came out.

"Ellen? What's going on? You at a bar?" He sounded miffed.

Good.

She hurried from the room, slipping into the basement to her living room and closing her apartment door on the merriment.

"No," she said, taking pleasure in saying what she

was about to say. "My parents are having a cocktail party." She laughed carelessly to show how amused she was by the whole thing. "They wanted me to meet their friends' eligible sons. My mother wants me to settle down. As if." She lowered her voice conspiratorially, savouring the darts she flung at him through the phone line. "But I've brought my own date to this shindig."

She sipped her wine as she paced the room. Why did she play this game? *Katrina, that's why. He's dating Katrina.*

"You have a date?" He paused a breath and added, "That's great." It sounded more like enthusiasm than sarcasm, which poked her ego.

"Well? To what do I owe the pleasure of this call? Don't tell me you're at home by yourself." Now, it was her turn to sound enthusiastic.

He chuckled. "Yes, but don't let it get around." His voice grew serious. "I'm actually working. From my office at home."

"Working on what? And what do you want from me?"

"I hate to intrude on your weekend, but I wanted to run something past you."

"Okay, I'll help if I can."

"How do you funnel money into an account and make it untraceable?"

His question jolted her to a halt, and she dropped to a seat on the couch. The moment the snoozing Mister Cuddles sensed her presence, he rose, stretched, and rubbed up against her. Absently, she set her wineglass on the floor and stroked the cat's soft fur until he jumped down and traipsed toward the kitchen and his food dish.

When the shock of what he'd asked passed, she

broke the silence. "Gabe, what did you find?" But she already knew the answer to that, because if it were nothing, he wouldn't have called her.

"Automatic transfers were set up for some accounts. I'm certain this transfers to an account maybe out of the country," Gabriel said.

"I thought you were going to let me look into this?" Ellen replied, annoyed he'd been doing her job.

"Yeah, but it's my company. I couldn't let it sit all weekend."

"It could take us weeks to ferret out every suspicious transaction from the entire two years or more. If it was Fran doing the transfers, the activity would've ceased on that account anyway."

"I know. Except someone transferred last night. If Fran set up the account, she wasn't the only one to have access to it. She might be innocent, or she might have an accomplice. The accomplice would make a likely suspect in her murder, Ellen."

CHAPTER 11

Ellen pulled the phone away from her ear and put the call on speaker. She told Gabriel she'd done that and let him know no one else was in the room.

"She could've created a Swiss bank account or something in the Caymans or elsewhere. One good thing about this is that to transfer the money you have to specify the account you're transferring it to." She contemplated how to avoid that. "Unless she transfers it more than once. So, once to the first account, which could be a shell corporation, then to another account we can't have access to, and then to the offshore account."

"I haven't found out where the money transfers to, but it would make sense for it to be a multi-step process, especially if she had an accomplice."

"Gabe, you're assuming it's Fran who stole the money."

"Ellen—"

"It likely was Fran," she cut in. "But you can't accuse her without evidence. What if she uncovered the thefts, so the real thief killed her?"

"I hadn't thought about it like that."

Reluctantly, she added, "It probably was Fran. No one else had that kind of access to those accounts. She had complete control and autonomy. You need to trust the person you hire when you offload that function. Business owners don't want to delve into the books. They want to run their businesses, so they hire controllers. It's a convenience and a risk. I'm sorry, Gabe."

"What for?"

"For everything that happened. What a domino effect from one night of sex!"

"I don't understand what you mean."

She almost told him right then that she'd left BRI because he'd dumped her. It was right there, ready to spill out, when she thought better of it. "I don't mean anything. Rather, our lives would be different, at any rate, if we either hadn't slept together then or we'd played things differently." She hoped that was answer enough to satisfy him.

It wasn't.

"Are you blaming us for what happened to Fran?"

"Of course not."

"Then what?"

"Nothing. An observation. More of a regret. I wish none of it would've happened—especially sleeping with you."

A protracted silence during which she regretted every word she'd said hovered between them. If only this weren't a phone conversation and she could see his face—something she'd see soon enough on Monday morning. If she didn't fix the error now, Monday morning would be hellacious.

"I didn't mean that."

When he didn't answer immediately, she feared the damage was irreparable. Then, he sighed and said, "I don't blame you for being bitter. You didn't deserve to have things end the way they did."

"We needn't review it."

"I'm trying to make a point here."

She nodded, even though he couldn't see it, and waited for him to continue.

"Don't blame us for what happened after that, Ellen. Nothing we did after that night can take away what we felt for each other then, and if things derailed afterwards, it had nothing to do with what Fran did or didn't do. She chose to embezzle from the company. That's on her and her accomplice."

"But if I hadn't left, she never would've worked there."

He paused a beat and then said, his voice gentle, "Did you leave so you wouldn't have to see me when I returned?"

She didn't hesitate this time. "Yes."

"And then I didn't come home anyway."

"So I left for no reason, and because I left, they hired Fran. You know the rest."

"For God's sake, you could've left for a hundred different reasons. That just happened to be the one that got you out the door and Fran in. You're not responsible for hiring her or for her choices, so stop feeling guilty about it. You want to do something positive, help me figure this out."

"I said I would." And then she'd leave. She needed out, away from him. But what if by leaving, she simply repeated past mistakes? Did flight always have to be her go-to response? She couldn't answer that. At least, for now, she'd stick around and help him clean up what she indirectly considered her mess, whether or not he believed it.

"Go enjoy your party. I'll see you Monday. Will you be all right?"

Someone rapped on her apartment door, and Rhonda called out, "Ellen? Are you in there?"

To Gabriel, Ellen said, her voice low and conspiratorial, "I'll be fine. Gotta go." She took him off speaker as he bid her goodbye and disconnected the call.

To Rhonda, she called out, "It's open; come on in."

As the door opened and Rhonda stepped into the living room, Ellen pasted a smile on her face. "Hey, what's up?"

"You tell me," Rhonda replied. "You're the one who disappeared from the party. John's wondering what he did wrong."

"It's all right. I'm coming back now. I got a work call."

"That wasn't a 'work' call," Rhonda retorted, air-quoting the word work. "That was Gabriel, and he's trying to horn in on your weekend."

"It was Gabe, yes, but he wanted to discuss work. He's been digging into the BRI financials and discovered suspicious fund transfers he wants me to look at." She'd revealed too much information, but in her great need to refute what Rhonda suspected, she couldn't stop herself. "Don't say anything to anyone. It's not for sure. I'll have to take a look on Monday, but at least it gives me a starting point." She sighed. "What happened to Francesca wasn't suicide. I'm sure of it, but we can't prove it."

"The media reports said the police were

investigating the death as suspicious."

"Yes, because it was likely murder. They just don't want to come out and say so yet."

"Have they talked to you?"

"No, but I'm probably low on the list they have to cover. I worked with her for two weeks and haven't had contact with her since I left. I wouldn't have much to offer in the way of insights into her death, especially if they think it might be suicide."

"Forget about it for now," Rhonda suggested. "Enjoy the party. Assure John he hasn't ticked you off. I could use another drink. How about you?"

"Sure," Ellen replied. "I'll be right up."

When Rhonda frowned, Ellen said, "I'm going to use the bathroom down here before I come up. Just go." She waved her friend along, and Rhonda obligingly left, shutting the door behind her.

Ellen locked the door and called Gabriel back. When he picked up, she said, "Have you looked at Fran's HR files? Her previous workplaces?"

"No." Her point must have dawned on him then, because he said, "I'll hunt them up tomorrow and let you know what I find."

Happy she'd helped him, even if minimally, Ellen said goodbye and disconnected the call. Time to return to the party.

***

"Glad you could join us. I've brought you a glass of wine. Red. I noticed that's what you usually drink." John held a wineglass out to Ellen, and she accepted it with a "thank you."

Not wanting to go into details but wishing to allay

his insecurities, she said, "Phone call. Work-related. Sorry I skipped out on you. Shall we go sit in the living room?"

"Sure." He allowed her to lead him to a couple of empty chairs in the living room. "Your parents have a nice house."

"Thanks. I'm only living here temporarily." Her expression turned sheepish. "I had a rough time a few years ago and moved back in. I'm picking myself back up to the point where I can think about moving out again in a year or two." She didn't want to leave too quickly. Once she left, she didn't plan to return.

"What happened? If you don't mind talking about it."

She contemplated what to tell him. "I had a bad breakup and then was unemployed for six weeks. Since I'd been living paycheque to paycheque, I had to give up my apartment and move back home. I'm lucky to have my parents as a fallback."

"Sure. Were you working as an accounting tech at the time?"

"Yes." She left it at that, but he pressed her.

"Where were you working?"

"Business Reports."

His eyes lit up. "Weren't they recently bought out?"

"Yes."

"I've heard they've had some tough times in the past few years. Maybe they couldn't get along without you." He chuckled.

She smiled, but it was a fake one; inside, tension bloomed and she had a craving for something to eat. "Want some food? My parents have quite a spread in the dining room. Have you seen it?"

He agreed, and they relocated to the buffet table.

71

Ellen piled her plate with samples of most of the available snacks, both salty and sweet. When they returned to their seats, she opened the conversation so he wouldn't get the opportunity to ask anything more about BRI or Gabriel or the past three years.

"So, what are you working on these days? Have you been with your current firm long?"

"I've been here about five years. I'm working toward saving money to open my own office."

"What's the name of the firm where you're working?" She didn't know one law firm from another, but she needed to keep him talking about himself.

"Benson, Dwyer, and Lawson."

As she'd expected, she'd never heard of them. "They keeping you busy?"

"Sure. Lots of labour-related disputes, mostly over severance pay."

"Is that what you specialize in?"

"Kind of by default. Sometimes, I represent the company; other times, the employee. Either way, I get the job done. I win my cases."

"Impressive." *He must be good if he wins all the time.* Or he exaggerated.

"Thanks. Do you know Gabriel Duncan?"

Damn, she'd let him get a word in.

"Sure. I knew him from BRI." She hesitated, not wanting to reveal they worked together once again, but decided there was no point in concealing the information. He'd find out soon enough. "He's also my new client."

He set the fork down on his plate and used a napkin to blot his mouth and wipe his fingers. "Interesting." He dropped the used napkin onto his plate.

"You know him?" It wouldn't surprise her. Gabriel

72

had a lot of connections through business and his family.

"No, just heard about the buyout and then that employee's death on the news. Terrible what happened."

"Yes."

"I heard it was suicide."

She shrugged, reluctant to discuss anything about Gabriel, Francesca, or her death. She didn't know anything anyway, and the police hadn't found her worthy of questioning. *Yet.*

"As far as I know, that's what they believe." A small lie wouldn't hurt. She bit into a cupcake, chewed, swallowed, ate some potato chips. Followed that up with nachos and salsa.

He grinned. "Enough talk about horrible things. We're here to have a good time. How about you give me a private tour of your apartment? I'd love to see it."

She hesitated, not sure she wanted to show him her private space, but it would help demonstrate to anyone who noticed them leave that he was her boyfriend. She stood and offered him her hand. "Sure, why not?"

***

"So," she said to John as they stepped into her apartment, "I hope you didn't let the cat out of the bag that you're my fake date for the night when my parents grilled you."

"Not at all," he replied. "I made it clear I'm interested in seeing you regularly. Your mother seemed delighted."

"And my father?"

"He's inscrutable. He smiled and nodded. I get the

feeling he trusts your judgment."

She laughed. "He does. Which means he might realize this is all a ruse to get my mother to back off."

She swept her arm around the living room and said, "Living room." Without waiting to see his reaction, she threw open the bathroom door. "Bathroom. Pretty big for a basement, and it's four-piece." She flicked the light on, waited for him to peer in, and flicked the light off again. From there, she directed him through an open door on the left to view the kitchen, which also was fairly large.

A fridge and stove stood against the south wall. Mister Cuddles's food dish, empty, sat, along with the water dish, on a placemat on the floor next to the fridge. Since the cat was nowhere in sight, she assumed he'd hid when he realized she'd brought a stranger into the apartment. The west wall had the double sink and cupboards above and below it, as well as a dishwasher to the right of the sink. The north wall had a bar with stools set underneath the windows. An island with more storage space underneath stood in the middle of the room.

"Well, that's the main living areas." She hesitated, suddenly not wanting to lead him through her bedroom. *Nonsense. It's just another room, and nothing really personal's on display.*

"Nice. Sparsely furnished, but it makes the rooms look bigger. I like the sectional sofa and the gas fireplace. You're lucky you have your own thermostat so you can control the heat setting."

"Yes, but I don't have any control over the air conditioning. It's always cold down here in the summer." She strode back through the kitchen, across the living room, and into her bedroom through its open door. He followed closely behind her.

She pointed to the double doors of her closet. "It's a walk-in. With a light in it." She flicked the light on in the bedroom to illuminate the entire room but kept the closet doors closed.

As she scanned the room, she tried to view it from a stranger's perspective: the desk, her laptop open on top of it nearest the closet; bookshelves along the wall; a queen bed sticking out into the centre of the room from the narrow end of the long room; and pale yellow walls that gave the room a touch of cheer.

"I wasn't lying, Ellen." His voice had grown quiet. "I do want to keep seeing you."

She shook her head. "We're friends, John."

"For now?"

She didn't want to promise him anything, but she also didn't want to offend him, so she simply said, "Yes, for now." While she didn't believe he was the dangerous stalker type, you couldn't tell with some guys. Best to be cagey about these things.

"Come on. We should go back upstairs before my dad comes searching for us." She smiled to show all was well and led the way back out of the apartment.

CHAPTER 12

Monday morning dawned snowy and cold. A typical late November day, according to the weather report. Gabriel drove to the office despite the dicey road conditions. He assumed the day would be a long one, and he didn't want to take public transit or a cab home. In the back of his mind, he also hoped to offer Ellen a ride home. Time to take their relationship to the next level—or to any level. He'd wasted enough time apart from her for a colossally stupid reason.

Not that it mattered, but he'd dug up the HR files from three years ago and pulled up a list of all the female employees who worked at BRI the day he and Ellen had hooked up. To be thorough, he'd also pulled up a client list that included all females who'd had meetings at the company offices that day. Luckily, that list turned out to be zero, so he could be relatively certain the mystery gossip worked at the company. The list, he was dismayed to note, included Katrina Weever, and after serious contemplation, she became his prime suspect.

He'd always been aware she was attracted to him, and until he'd returned from England, he hadn't given her too much thought. She was nice enough, attractive, smart, but back then, Ellen preoccupied him. Their relationship appeared to be moving forward, had seemed solid and full of potential. Why would he let another woman distract him?

The rumour of a fiancé was a perfect way to force him to doubt Ellen and her relationship with him though it was also stupid and risky. If he'd tracked down Ellen immediately, she'd have denied the rumour, and they'd have started dating again a year ago.

So, why hadn't he?

Because the fiancé deception had worked. The moment he heard it, he reacted with jealous rage and wanted to lash out at Ellen to soothe his bruised ego. If she'd married another man and started a family with him, Gabriel didn't want to know about it. Denying he'd wanted to find her again helped him avoid the grief he felt at losing her to someone else. As far as Katrina getting Gabriel for herself, if that had been the point of all this, it worked: he'd started dating her. She'd been more than happy to reconnect with him as soon as he returned. She'd called him, as a matter of fact, the day after he'd settled back into his apartment.

He never even asked her how she knew he was back. Didn't think about how quickly she'd found him. Didn't ask her what she knew about Ellen, who never bothered to keep tabs on him the way Katrina had. But then, Ellen had her own reasons for wanting to forget his very existence.

His assistant buzzed him then, ripping him from his reveries, and told him Ellen had arrived for their meeting. A moment after he gave permission to send her in, there was a tap at his door. When it opened, she entered, wearing a tailored navy pantsuit with a blouse in pale pink. Her hair cascaded in loose curls over her shoulders. He'd always loved it when she wore it down like that. She often tied it back when she worked, which accentuated her high cheekbones and almond-shaped eyes, but he loved to see those tresses loose and flowing.

Christ, if I don't control myself, I'm going to grab her and kiss her, and she'll file a sexual harassment complaint against me.

He rose to greet her, and she smiled shyly as she shut the door behind her.

Lock it popped into his head, but instead of vocalizing it and embarrassing himself, he pressed the intercom button and asked his assistant to get them coffee. The prospect of the devout Catholic Mrs. Carbajal catching them in a passionate clench should keep him in line.

"How are you?" Ellen asked. She seated herself in one of the two chairs in front of his desk and crossed her legs. She set her laptop bag next to the chair.

"I'm fine. Did you have a good weekend? How was the party?" *Did you sleep with your date?*

"Good. I managed to avoid any romantic entanglements with anyone—for the most part."

He froze, his mind going blank. "For the most part?"

She beamed a smile at him. "My date let me know he might be interested in more than that."

"What did you tell him?"

She waved a hand dismissively. "No promises. We'll see where it goes."

He scowled. *Is this retribution for my date with Katrina?*

If it was, he could handle it. There'd be no more dates with Katrina—not if he could get Ellen to agree she'd have no more dates, even fake ones, with her mystery man.

Ellen's expression grew serious then, and a sinking sensation in his gut heralded she had news he didn't want to hear. He waited her out with bated breath.

"I need to ask you something," she began.

"Shoot." He leaned back in his chair, folded his hands in his lap, and crossed his legs at the ankles, a display of nonchalance he didn't feel.

"You said someone told you I was engaged. Who was it?"

"A friend." He refused to reveal his source. She'd get angry with Carl, and that wouldn't help anyone. "Why?"

Ellen blinked, and her lips parted in surprise. "Why wouldn't I want to know who spread lies about me?"

"What difference does it make? That happened last year," he said. "I asked about you when I returned to BRI and discovered you'd left. Someone said you'd quit when you got engaged."

"And you believed it."

Gabriel sat up, his back rigid. "Why would someone make that up?" But he knew—or at least suspected.

"That's an excellent question—one I'd like answered, which is why you need to tell me who told you."

He met her gaze steadily. "One of the marketing clients. He said he heard it from one of the programmers. Couldn't recall who."

She frowned, but her expression was more puzzled than angry. "How the hell would a rumour like that even start? I gave my notice, trained Fran, and left. I never told anyone I was leaving to get married. What the hell would getting engaged have to do with me quitting my job even if it was true?"

He shrugged. "I don't understand it either. Let's drop it, okay? My marketing buddy said she left the company anyway." Another fact that pointed the finger in Katrina's direction.

A tap sounded on the door. It opened, and Mrs. Carbajal peeked into the room. "Your coffee, Mr. Duncan."

Relieved by the interruption, Gabriel waved her in. He'd take the few minutes she used to serve the coffee and think about how to handle Ellen. Somehow, he had to turn this around. Now, more than ever, he determined to take her home at the end of the day. He refused to have their one night together be their only night together.

CHAPTER 13

The stunned look on Gabriel's face when she told him the date she'd invited to her parents' party wanted more than a pretend relationship gratified her. Sure, the stunt was immature, but sometimes, a tiny vengeance was better than no vengeance. She didn't intend to hurt Gabriel, just to make him feel as if she were as in demand as he was. If she poked him, she could force him to reveal how serious he was with Katrina Weever.

As the name flashed through Ellen's mind, her eyes narrowed. Katrina was not right for Gabriel. If he no longer wanted Ellen, she could get over that, but not if he moved on from her to Katrina Weever.

Ellen couldn't say exactly what about the software developer made her insides churn, she just knew the woman would make Gabriel miserable in the long run. In truth, Ellen wanted him to be happy even if it couldn't be with her, and he would never be happy with someone like Katrina.

When Mrs. Carbajal left the room again, Ellen picked up the coffee the assistant had served her and sipped. She considered helping herself to a cookie from a mounded plate of them, but she left them untouched. A protracted silence blanketed the room, and she allowed it to stretch. She needed Gabriel to be the one to break it. How else would she learn his priorities, learn what he wanted from her?

Gabriel, who'd also picked up his coffee and sipped it, set his cup and saucer down and caved. "All right. How do we resolve this?"

What does that mean? Ellen set her cup and saucer down and replied, "Resolve what?"

He scowled. "Come on, Ellen, you know what I mean. This ridiculous game we're both playing."

"What do you expect from me, Gabe?"

"Nothing you're not willing to give. Honesty would be a nice start."

"Honesty." She rose and paced the room. "That's swell coming from you." She whirled on him. "How are things with Katrina?"

Smugness flashed across his face, so fleetingly she wasn't sure she'd interpreted it correctly.

"Katrina's fine. I went out with her three, maybe four, times."

Ellen halted her pacing and glared at him. "How long have you been back in the country?"

"About a year."

So, he and Katrina had gone out as much as four times in the past roughly twelve months. Not too frequently to indicate the relationship was serious but enough to show an interest in her on his part. Katrina had had a thing for him three years ago. The realization dawned on Ellen that Katrina was likely the mystery gossip. It made sense. A risky, immature stunt like that was more likely to come from someone in her twenties who suffered from a raging crush.

"Okay. You didn't have a serious relationship in England or you wouldn't be seeing Katrina," Ellen observed. She vocalized it even though she risked making herself vulnerable to him by doing so. "How serious are you and Katrina?"

"Not at all serious. The last time we parted company, I told her I didn't want to lead her on—that I just wanted to be friends."

"Ouch. Did you say 'it's not you, it's me'? That's a classic."

He gave her a stricken look and rose from his chair. "I didn't want to hurt her, but I'm not interested in a serious relationship with her." He strode out from behind his desk to stand in front of Ellen. Before she could react, he took her hands in his. "Ever since we ran into each other in Carol's office, I've thought about you constantly. I can't sleep for thinking about you. How's that for honest? You can't deny you feel something for me still. We had something special, and I still feel it."

She tugged on her hands, but he held them firmly in his.

"Answer me. If you can say you feel nothing for me, that you don't want to have anything to do with me, I'll release you, and we'll keep our relationship professional."

Ellen's heart pounded. She wanted to give him another chance—craved it like she craved food right now. "Did you sleep with her?"

"It's my business if I had, but no, we never slept together. It's been three years since I've slept with anyone."

She'd been his last partner. Ellen released a sigh

along with the tension she'd been holding inside. "I haven't either." She hoped that admission would be enough, that he wouldn't want to question her about John, but, once again, she was disappointed. Gabriel wasn't about to let her get away with hiding anything from him.

"This John person. How serious is it? You may not have slept with him, but you're dating him."

She averted her eyes, unable to meet his gaze. "I'm not dating him. He came to the party as my fake date so my parents would get off my back about finding a boyfriend. My mother thinks I'll be unhappy without one." Her mother wasn't too far off the mark. Ellen's unhappiness wasn't so much the result of not having a boyfriend as it was the result of not having Gabriel. The revelation hit her like a body slam.

"You told me he was your date."

"Yes, I did." Her eyes welled up as conflicting emotions flooded through her. Gabriel had abandoned her, and when he returned, he not only didn't look her up, but he also started dating the woman who'd probably spread rumours about Ellen to keep Gabriel out of her life. That he hadn't known she'd come between them was irrelevant. She'd manipulated him into sabotaging the best relationship either of them had ever had. She tugged at her hands again, more roughly this time, but he still held them firmly in his grasp.

"To make me jealous?"

She remained silent, unsure how to respond to that. *Yes, to make you jealous. To make you think you'd lose me. So you'd want to fight for me.*

None of those options made her look good. Admitting any of those things would probably make him sorry he'd started down this path. He'd dump her again.

"If it helps you, your strategy worked," he said. "I got good and steamed Saturday night." With a finger under her chin, he angled her head so their gazes locked. "I didn't sleep at all."

She tried to chuckle, but it sounded more like a hiccough caught on a sob.

"I was jealous of Katrina," she admitted. If he'd been willing to expose his ego, the least she could do was match him revelation for revelation. And it allowed her to dodge the original question.

"Ellen ..." His voice trailed off, but she relished the sound of her name in that husky baritone. It showed her she wasn't the only one overwhelmed by emotion.

An ache filled her body, and her lips tingled. *Kiss me.* But she couldn't say it out loud. *Please kiss me.* She pleaded with him with her eyes and parted her lips.

"Do you feel something for me, Ellen? Answer me, yes or no."

"Yes."

The moment he heard the word, he drew her into his body. His arms wrapped around her, and his mouth dived to hers. She accepted him with a low moan, tasting him, drawing his breath into her soul.

She didn't know how long they kissed, only that, while they did, time stood still and her heart sped up. Their bodies pressed together as if they wanted to fuse, and desire flared up within and through her. Her arms had wrapped around him without her noticing, but now, she moved her hands up along his back, over his shoulders. She slid them into his hair, sifting its softness through her fingers. The need to touch him all over demanded to be satisfied, and she responded to the call.

Ellen didn't come up for air until a knock at the door dragged her from the depths with a gasp. Gabriel released her, and she threw herself into her chair. By the time he opened the door to Mrs. Carbajal, Ellen had slowed her breaths though her heart still triphammered. Gabriel, looking a little rumpled and flushed, asked his assistant what she wanted.

"Detective Morris is down in the lobby," the woman replied, her gaze raking over his mussed hair. "Shall I send him up? He's asking for Miss Haddigan."

"Did you tell him she was here?"

"Yes, sir. I won't lie to the police."

"I wouldn't ask you to." He said it breezily. Ellen sensed a casual rapport between boss and employee that surprised her, considering he hadn't been the woman's boss for long.

Maybe because he was a client here before he became the owner. She remembered joking with him herself within days of their meeting. He'd been a charmer, always.

"Send him up."

Mrs. Carbajal vanished and Gabriel closed the door.

"If he's going to question you, I'm going to have him do it here with me."

"Are you worried I might say something wrong?"

He shook his head. "Does it bother you to have me present?"

"No. I think I'd feel better if you were." At least, she thought she'd feel better with him here. When the knock sounded on the door, Ellen's hands gripped the arms of her chair. Suddenly, she didn't want to talk to the detective at all.

CHAPTER 14

Gabriel let the detective into the room and introduced him to Ellen, who offered her hand and a firm handshake. Mrs. Carbajal returned with a cup and saucer for the detective, poured him a cup of coffee, and left. Morris angled the chair beside Ellen so it faced her and sat in it. Preliminaries done, he established Gabriel wanted to stay in the room and that Ellen agreed to this. Morris got right to the point.

"Miss Haddigan, I was told by the head of HR you haven't worked at BRI for almost three years, but when you did, you were the one to train Miss Newton. Is that correct?"

"Yes. I had nothing to do with hiring her, but I worked with her for the two weeks I remained here after she came on board."

"How'd she do?"

"Fine; otherwise, I'd have let them know they needed to find someone else, and they'd have let her go. She did good work and got up to speed quickly."

"Any problems with clients?"

Ellen didn't hesitate. "None. She was friendly, good with people. Clients liked and trusted her. She had a knack for getting them to pay their invoices on time. I thought she'd work out well." She thought back on that time. Was there anything at all that might have alerted her to the possibility of Francesca stealing from the company? She couldn't think of anything.

"I understand you're taking over the financials here once again."

"That's correct." Ellen glanced at Gabriel. He calmly sipped his coffee, his posture relaxed. She set her cup and saucer on the desk and sat back in her chair. To keep herself from grabbing the plate of cookies, setting it on her thighs, and devouring them all, she folded her hands in her lap.

"Have you gone through the files yet?"

Keeping her gaze level, forcing herself not to glance again at Gabriel, she said, "No." That was true. She'd only logged into the system at By the Books and given the account a cursory review.

"When will you do that?"

"That's why I'm here today. It'll take me a while to go through everything, and I wanted to do it from here. Francesca would've filed hard copies of a lot of the transactions. I need to look at them and make sure they all line up."

"How long will that take?" Detective Morris swiped a cream-filled chocolate cookie and ate it in two bites.

"Weeks, probably. I'm not sure how many. Two might be enough."

He contemplated her while he finished chewing. After a moment, he said, "What have you done with the account so far?"

"I've set it up at By the Books so it's in our system

and logged into the financials here remotely. I examined some of it as I went along, but I haven't done any deep dives into it." Here's where he could dig deeper and learn of her suspicions. She didn't want to keep anything from the police. If he asked, she'd tell the truth.

"Notice anything odd?"

"An increase in expenses and payouts to contractors I hadn't seen before. I can't say if that's odd or not. That's why I have to go through hard copies here. It might be something; it might be nothing."

"I see." He pondered in silence.

Ellen risked a glance at Gabriel. His gaze remained fixed on the detective, his expression neutral.

Morris set his cup and saucer down and rose. "I'd like to talk to you again when you've reviewed all the files. Would that be all right?" He addressed first Ellen and then Gabriel.

Gabriel answered him. "Sure. When Ellen has completed her review, I'll call you myself."

They rose. Morris took a business card holder from his pocket and gave them each a card. As he passed it to Gabriel, he said, "In case you lost the other one." He snatched another cookie from the plate and turned to leave. "If either of you thinks of anything else, please let me know."

After the detective left, Gabriel said, "I'll show you to Francesca's old office. You can work there."

Her expression must have betrayed her hurt and puzzlement, because he moved to her side and said, "We'll discuss everything after work if you'll let me take you to dinner."

Butterfly wings fluttered in her solar plexus.

"Okay."

"I'm not avoiding anything. We need to find out what happened."

"You're not angry with anything I said?"

His eyes widened as he processed what her question implied. "No. You told the truth. I expected nothing less."

"I didn't want to tell him everything about what we suspect. It might not be true."

"You did fine. You're not hiding anything. There's nothing to tell."

Feeling lighter than she had since Gabriel reappeared in her life, Ellen followed him to Francesca's office and got to work.

***

At lunchtime, Ellen slipped from the office and grabbed a quick bite at the deli down the street. She hadn't seen Gabriel all day and, quite frankly, needed the time to think. In the sandwich shop, she ran into Carl Walker, and when he invited her to sit with him, she agreed. She set her tray across from him on the table, and once she removed her coat and draped it over her chair, she sat down.

"Haven't seen you in a while, Carl. How are you?"

"Fine, thanks. You?"

"I'm good. You visiting BRI today?"

He shook his head and took a slurp of whatever dark soft drink he had in the cup in front of him before he replied. "I'm next door. I might pop into BRI to check in on the accounts and say hi to Gabe. I hear he's there today—will probably be here every day for the foreseeable future."

"Yes."

"You working together now?"

She ignored the question as something occurred to her. "Have you visited BRI over the last three years?"

"Yeah, regularly. Why?"

"So, you knew Francesca Newton?"

"Sure. Shame about what happened to her."

Ellen nodded and bit into her pastrami sandwich. She chewed in silence, hoping he'd fill the void with chatter about the dead woman, and he did just that.

"I saw her that last day she worked at BRI, actually." He sipped his drink again before continuing. "She looked fine, you know? Not like someone about to go home and off herself. That happened a week later, but still, she couldn't have gotten that depressed in one week."

"Did she ever strike you as someone who was depressed?"

"Never."

"Stressed?"

"No. Well, not more than anyone would be when they worked on finances and had deadlines to meet. She had problems, but I didn't think she had serious problems."

"Did you ever go out with her?"

"You mean like on a date?"

"Well, no. She was married, wasn't she?"

"Yeah, so we kept it friendly. Had lunch in this very deli sometimes. She was fun. Good to hang out with but not my type."

What was Carl's type? Why even mention a type if she was unavailable? Did Carl think her too young? He was the same age as Gabriel—thirty-four. Francesca had been what? Twenty-three? Twenty-four at the most. Katrina wasn't much older, something else to infuriate Ellen about the other woman's relationship with Gabriel. Katrina was twenty-six, and while the age difference shouldn't matter, to Ellen it did, mostly because it was Katrina and Gabriel. She shook off those thoughts and returned to her conversation with Carl.

"She ever confide in you?"

Instead of answering the question, Carl studied her in silence and then said, "What's with the third degree?"

"I'm curious. Carl, I'm digging through a dead woman's work. I would like to understand what happened to her. It's ... unnerving."

"All right. No, she didn't confide in me about her work, if that's what you're asking."

Ellen stared at her plate for a moment, then raised her head to meet his gaze. "Did she ever confide in you about her personal life?"

"I don't know if I feel comfortable answering that question."

"I'm not asking you to betray a confidence or to gossip about her."

"Then what? Because that's how it feels to me." He'd finished his food and looked as if he wanted to flee the scene.

"Either something made her kill herself or ..." She couldn't bring herself to say someone might have killed Francesca. Murdered her. It was surreal to know a murder victim. "If there's something that could help the police ... Did you have lunch with her often? She consider you a friend?"

"Don't push it, Ellen." He stood. "I've got to go."

"Wait! Just wait!"

He glared at her. "I'd say it was nice catching up, but it really wasn't."

"Tell me this: did you hear from her after Gabriel fired her?"

He slowly sat down again. "Yeah."

She waited, afraid that if she pressed him, he'd clam up.

His face scrunched up as if he'd tasted something sour. "You want to help her?"

"Yes," she whispered.

"She called me at work the day she died."

Ellen sucked in a breath and held it.

"Said she wanted to meet. We were going to meet at a coffee shop near her apartment."

She let the breath out. "What happened?"

"I went to meet her, and she never showed."

Ellen didn't ask why Francesca never showed. They both knew the answer to that.

CHAPTER 15

For the rest of the afternoon Ellen kept her head down and her face in BRI's financial data. By the time Gabriel ducked his head into the office to ask her if she was ready to leave, she still had at least ten days' worth of work ahead of her. But she set everything aside, organized the file folders she'd pulled from the file cabinet, and arranged them so she could pick it all up where she'd left off in the morning.

Gabriel helped her with her coat, and they made small talk as they locked her office door and walked to the elevator. By some unspoken agreement, neither brought up the subject of Francesca, her death, or suspicious activity in the accounts. They kept the conversation light, casual. If they touched on BRI, it was superficial observations about the corporate culture or the various people who worked there, most of whom Ellen had worked with in the past. Ellen also made sure not to steer the conversation to Katrina or to Carl, but she intended to broach both as a topic of conversation once they'd settled in at the restaurant.

To her surprise, Gabriel led her to his car in the underground parking.

"Aren't we walking to Foundation?" she asked when he pressed the garage button on the elevator down.

"No, I thought we'd check out this new Italian restaurant near my place."

"Where might that be?" She'd never had the opportunity to see his place. He'd had an apartment on Lake Shore Boulevard before he'd left for England, but she didn't want to assume he still lived there.

"Still on Lake Shore. The restaurant is close to my place. We can park in the underground at my apartment complex and walk down."

"I'm not going back to your place after," she warned.

"I'm not expecting you to. We'll have a nice dinner together, talk about what we both want, and then, you can grab a cab home."

They reached his BMW, and he opened the door for her. She slid into the seat and made herself comfortable. The car still had that new smell, which told her he'd bought it when he returned from England.

The driver's door opened and Gabriel climbed in.

"We never had the chance to catch up," she said. "How were things in England? What was it like?"

He told her as they drove to the restaurant, and she got the impression he'd enjoyed working there.

"The people were great. Not so much the weather though. Rained a lot more there than it does here. Less snow all around, which is a plus." He laughed.

"Did you stay in touch with people at BRI?" It hadn't occurred to her he might, but it would make

95

sense.

"Yes. If I needed overflow programmers, a practical solution was to call on them. The British pound is better than the Canadian dollar, so I got a deal when you factor in the exchange."

She thought about how that connected to the work she was doing and what invoices she should look at. "Did you deal with Francesca?"

"No. I had a controller who handled invoices. My job's more high-level than that, Ellen. I don't handle the details."

"You heard nothing from or about her? I'm trying to get a feel for her day-to-day activities and how everything flowed. I'll take care of your invoices and billing, no problem—I remember well how everything worked, and it hasn't changed too much since I was last here. But I want to understand how she worked. Her routine. I'll also have to interview the clients she talked to, the vendors she billed."

"I understand, but I really can't help you with that."

"Who could?"

As he pondered, she checked out the surroundings. They'd arrived at Lake Shore, and she peered out over Lake Ontario. Grey clouds loomed heavy over everything, and the water crashed into the shore, spewing up froth. No ice had formed over any of it yet, but it all looked cold and dreary.

"The clients and vendors are easy enough."

"Yes," she agreed. "There are records of those, but if some are fake, I'll want to talk to anyone at BRI who might have had anything to do with submitting invoices. Who took over for her when she went on vacation, for example?"

He stared at her, surprise on his face. "I don't know.

I've never known her to take time off."

"I'll verify with HR, but that seems odd to me."

Why would Francesca never take a vacation in three years? *I should ask her husband.*

***

They sat across from each other at a table for two in a cozy Italian restaurant with dark wood, soft lighting from wall sconces, and flickering candles on the tables. Piano music played lightly in the background. Each had a glass of wine in front of them and a bottle of Valpolicella between them. He'd normally consider the ambience romantic, except that Ellen had already broached the subject of Katrina, which took all the wind out of his romance sails.

"I suspect her of starting the rumour that I was engaged," Ellen finished.

He might as well be honest. "The thought crossed my mind too, but does it really matter?"

"I'm bringing it up not because I'm still grinding on your possible relationship with her. I'm bringing it up because maybe she was also Fran's accomplice."

That thought had also crossed his mind, but he'd discarded it as a possibility. "How did you draw that conclusion?"

"She probably wanted me out of BRI."

He shook his head, not agreeing with the logic. "That's a stretch. How in the world would she know that if we broke up you'd quit your job there? Besides, she had nothing to do with that, and you'd both left the company by the time I returned."

"Okay, but you continued to use BRI even while you were gone. Gabe, you hurt me enough I just wanted away."

His dismay must've been evident, because she hurriedly added, "It's fine now. I'm stating how it was then. That's what we need to hash out."

"All right. But that has nothing to do with Katrina," he said, forcing down visions of Ellen quitting her job to escape contact with him.

"If we hadn't broken up at all, I guess I would've stayed," she admitted. "Before you left, it never entered my mind to quit, so you're probably right, and Katrina only wanted me out of your life not out of the company. Now I think about it, if she wanted me out of the company, sabotaging me professionally would've made more sense. She never even said anything to you until you returned. That means she didn't want you looking me up to get back together."

"Agreed."

The waiter came and took their order. They both ordered a Caesar salad and decided to split a pizza. After arguing a bit, Gabriel caved and agreed to let her have pineapple on half. Who put pineapple on pizza? At least she didn't complain about the meat he wanted on it.

"I talked to Carl today at lunch," Ellen said. "He made an interesting comment about Fran."

"What's that?"

"He said she wasn't his type." Ellen picked up her napkin and spread it on her lap. "What's his type? Do you know?"

Gabriel mimicked her moves with his napkin but kept his gaze on her movements. When she raised her head, they locked eyes.

"Why would he care what type Fran was? She's married." His brain kicked in and reminded him he'd used the wrong tense. When he spoke again, his voice was soft. "*Was* married."

"I suppose that was his point. He didn't think of her in that way because she was married, but then he said she wasn't his type. Any idea what that is?" When he could only stare at her, she added, "I'm curious. About what a guy thinks is his type."

Gabriel contemplated the question. Should he reveal personal information about his friend? Was this any of her business? Perhaps. She was certainly in this with him, and if Carl had colluded with Francesca, Gabriel would be justified in talking about him. Besides, he wanted to be honest with Ellen, to confide in her. He could trust her because they were in this together. Finally, he spoke. "Carl always dated women older than him. Not always much older, sometimes just two, three, years. Five years, once." He recalled a woman even older than that, but he'd said enough for now. He'd made his point.

"Oh." She slanted Gabriel a look, and with her brows raised and her mouth quirked, she said, "What's your type?"

Without missing a beat, he replied, "Look in the mirror."

She laughed, but with relief. "I guess you're my type too."

He smiled but chased it with a frown. "Did Carl say anything else?"

She nodded. "He mentioned something you should know."

"What's that?"

The server arrived then with their salads, forcing a break in the conversation. They waited for him to set down the salads, offer them pepper and parmesan cheese, which both of them accepted, and walk away. Gabriel picked up his wine and sipped.

Ellen kept her gaze on him this time. "I don't know if he told you this, but he spoke to Fran the day she died. He said she wanted to meet with him."

Shock had Gabriel setting down his wineglass and leaning forward. "No, he never mentioned that." His good friend hadn't told him this critical piece of information. Yet he'd been more than happy to pass on the fake news that Ellen was engaged. A chill ran through him. "Did he say why she wanted to meet?"

"No. She didn't tell him, and she never showed up to the meeting." Her face pale, she met his gaze. "At least, that's what he said."

He picked up his wine and gulped it, but the warmth it flowed through him didn't ease his worry. Could Carl have had something to do with Francesca's death? Was it possible he'd been her accomplice? The more they dug into this, the more complicated it got, but he still didn't want to call Detective Morris with any of this stuff. No way would Gabriel drag his best friend into a murder investigation without proof he was involved in it.

"I guess I'd better have a word with my friend," Gabriel said.

CHAPTER 16

Ellen enjoyed the meal despite her work worries and a nagging feeling she was missing crucial information. Once they set aside the shop talk, they both relaxed into the dinner and conversation. The rest of the evening passed quickly, and before she realized it, Gabriel was paying the bill and she was shrugging into her coat.

When they reached the entrance to the restaurant, Ellen said, "I'll call a rideshare from here."

"You could walk back to my place, have a coffee."

"It's Monday. I don't want to stay out too late."

He looked as if he wanted to press the issue, but since she'd earlier told him emphatically that she wouldn't go home with him, he let it drop. The relief she felt over that surprised her. She'd expected to want to go back to his place and struggle over saying no.

As he waited with her in the restaurant's foyer for her ride to show up, he put his arm around her. "We never talked about that kiss."

Stunned, she realized they hadn't. It seemed so long

ago since it'd happened. "What did you want to say?"

"I'd like to do it again."

She leaned into him, tilting up her face to offer him her lips. He accepted the offer, pressing his mouth on hers gently. With the tip of his tongue, he explored and tasted. She released a small sigh and melted into him. They lost themselves in the moment until a horn blast from the street brought Ellen thudding back to reality.

She pulled away. "My ride." Her voice sounded thick and husky.

"All right. But I won't let you off so easy next time."

Smiling, she gave him a quick hug and said, "I'll see you tomorrow. Bright and early." She pushed through the door and headed for the car.

Once she'd settled in the back seat, she looked out the rear window at him. He stood watching from the sidewalk. When he noticed her staring, he waved to her, and as the car pulled away from the curb, she waved back. While they hadn't agreed out loud to start seeing one another again, Ellen was confident everything would be all right. Tonight, she was sure, she'd sleep well for the first time in three years.

***

Gabriel had almost reached the front entrance of his apartment building when he spotted the young woman standing in the shadows of the covered walkway leading to the entrance doors. The thought that she waited for someone crossed his mind, but he didn't realize she waited for him until she moved into the light when she spotted his approach.

Katrina.

He spoke first. "What are you doing here?" After

the surprise and shock at seeing her came the relief that Ellen wasn't with him.

She took a step toward him, staggered, and braced herself on the stone pillar beside her.

"Are you drunk?" Just what he needed right now. Well, he couldn't leave her out here, drunk and cold. He'd take her upstairs, sober her up, and then put her in a cab and send her home. For a moment, he considered pouring her into a cab as is, but he couldn't bring himself to do it. One look into her eyes and he could tell she was well sauced. To send her off on her own in this state would be irresponsible.

"Gabe." She laughed. "Gabe the babe. It rhymes. I bet I could make a poem with your name. Want me to try?"

"Christ, no." He gripped her by the upper arm and tried to lead her to the front doors, but she tripped, and he had to support her with both arms. He draped one of her arms around his neck—awkward, considering their height difference—and half-dragged, half-carried, her to the entrance. He fumbled in his pocket for the electronic key and, after further struggle with opening the door, finally had them as far as the lobby. With more effort, he had them in the elevator, where he faced the biggest challenge of his night so far: she threw herself at him, showering his face with kisses.

The mirrors in the elevator showed him in great comic relief fending off her advances. He laughed helplessly at first, but her hands had joined her lips. What she probably thought was hot and sexy turned quickly from comical to sad.

"Kat, quit it. I'll get you cleaned up, and then you're going home."

"You dumped me. I'd do anything for you, Gaby

baby. Why don't you love me?"

"We weren't ... you're not ..." He couldn't manage anything coherent, and what difference would it make anyway? She was well and truly snockered and wouldn't remember anything he said even an hour from now. He might as well wait until morning and reason with her then. Not that she'd be here in the morning. No way. He realized suddenly how quiet it was. When he looked down at her, she dangled at his side, unconscious.

Glorious.

They reached the penthouse, and he carried her from the elevator and down the hall to his corner unit. As he juggled her—and the purse she'd dropped when she'd passed out—while searching for his keys, his cell phone sounded.

Perfect. He ignored it.

Once he had her in his apartment, he kicked off his shoes in the foyer and carried her to the living room. He set her on the couch in a seated position. Out cold, she toppled over. He wouldn't be talking to her tonight nor would he be sending her home like this. Cursing, he slipped her shoes off—high-heeled pumps in the damn snow—and carried them to the tiled foyer where he placed them next to his shoes. Next, he removed her coat and set it and her purse on the armchair ninety degrees from the couch. He lifted her legs onto the couch and put one of the decorative pillows from the end under her head. At least it was flat and not one of the puffier ones he had on the sofa in the den.

Who cares? Just let this nightmare be over. When she woke in the morning, they would have a serious conversation.

For the first time since he'd had the place decorated,

he regretted the white carpeting. He rushed into the nearby powder room and grabbed a trash bin. It was almost full, so he changed it, and with a fresh bag in it, he set it on the floor below her face. He examined her carefully. She breathed deeply, evenly, which he assumed was a good sign. Strands of her strawberry-blonde hair lay plastered against her cheeks. Her lipstick had smeared, giving her mouth a clownish appearance. He contemplated getting a wet washcloth and cleaning her up a bit but was afraid if he tried that she'd wake up or, worse, wake up and puke.

How long should he let her sleep it off here? He remembered the missed call then and checked his phone.

Terrific. Ellen had called him. He checked for a message and listened to it.

"Hope you made it home okay. Just wanted to say thanks for tonight. See you tomorrow."

Should he call her back? He glanced at the unconscious woman on his sofa. If he did, would he have to tell her about Katrina? Would he ever have to tell her about Katrina?

Shit. How honest did a man have to be with the woman he probably loved? He considered calling Carl to ask for advice but changed his mind. Talking to Carl right now would come with its own problems.

In the end, Gabriel got Katrina a blanket and a glass of water, covered her with the blanket, and set the glass of water on the coffee table next to her. He left a night light on, and after locking the door to the apartment, he went into his bedroom. In case Katrina woke up and got any ideas about climbing into bed with him during the night, he locked the bedroom door. Satisfied he'd done all he could to safeguard his virtue and his guest's health, he washed up, got his pyjamas on, and went to bed.

***

"Cat on the balcony." The voice belongs to a dark-haired man Gabriel should recognize but doesn't. "She'll fly."

Gabriel attempts to stir, but his arms and legs weigh him down. He opens his mouth, but no words come out.

Cat got your tongue?

The man outside laughs. A woman, her voice mocking and familiar, jibber-jabbers, then falls silent.

Cat got her tongue.

Whooshing. Whooshing? What whooshes? It must be that drum rolling. Drum. Rolling. A drum rolls across the floor of his living room, but why does it sound like bare floor when he has wall-to-wall carpeting?

Gabriel stirred, the threads of the dream vanishing from his mind, and rolled over. Silence and fatigue lulled him back into another dream, on a beach, ocean waves lapping at his ankles. *He has to find a bathroom and* …

He roused and opened his eyes. Had he heard something, or was that the dream? He checked the time on his clock radio. Three o'clock. He lay back down and listened to the silence, trying to recall the sound he'd heard—if he'd actually heard a sound and hadn't dreamt it. A voice? The door? Something about a drum, but that made no sense.

He remembered his guest in the living room.

Better go check on her. The temptation to lie back down and fall asleep again almost had him doing just that, but he needed to take a piss—that dream made sense. He dragged himself up and slipped on his slippers.

Since all was quiet outside his bedroom door, he veered first into the en suite and relieved his bladder. After washing his hands, he'd awakened enough that if he returned to bed he'd just toss and turn, wondering if Katrina was okay. He threw on his robe.

The noise. A sound had awakened him; it hadn't been part of the dream. Had it? *A whoosh.*

When he opened his bedroom door and stepped into the hallway, an icy blast of air made him shiver and suck in his breath.

What the hell? She opened the balcony doors? Well, that explains the whoosh. He stormed into the living room, ready to confront her.

She wasn't on the couch where he'd left her, and as he'd deduced, the balcony doors yawned wide open.

"Katrina?" He strode to the balcony. "Kat?"

No sign of her. Had she left? The thin layer of powdery snow showed someone had walked to the railing, but the footprints had been obscured into a smooth, powdery trail. Still, he could see they weren't made by the small, delicate feet he'd removed shoes from the night before. He tiptoed in his slippers to the railing; his feet disturbed the snow, but he stayed far away from the original trail, a sensation of horror growing in the pit of his stomach.

He peered over the edge at the pool of streetlight splashing the walkway beneath his balcony. On the sidewalk, a woman lay on the ground, her body contorted, but he recognized the dress. Katrina's head was twisted to the side, and her arms and legs splayed out on the pavement.

Gabriel went inside to call 911.

CHAPTER 17

Tuesday morning Ellen arrived at the office in high spirits. She'd slept in but had made up the time by skipping breakfast and leaving the television off. That oversight began to haunt her the moment she stepped into the lobby and discovered the company receptionist, Karen, sobbing at her desk.

Ellen hurried to the woman's kiosk. "What happened? What's wrong?"

Karen met Ellen's gaze with a grimace of anguish. "Haven't you heard? Katrina's dead, and they've got Gabriel at the police station. They think he might have killed her."

Ellen staggered, and if she hadn't grabbed onto the counter, she'd have fallen. "What do you mean? Are you sure? How'd you hear this?"

Why hadn't she turned on the news this morning? She usually did, but she'd been in such a wonderful mood and in such a rush to get to work she'd skipped the depressing reports.

"I got a call from his assistant. She heard from

Gabe's lawyer."

"What else did she say?"

"Nothing. Just not to talk to reporters."

"Have you heard from reporters?"

Commotion at the entrance answered her question. A cluster of people with microphones and cameras pressed their way into the building. Ellen rushed to the elevators as security approached the scrum. She pressed the button repeatedly, futilely trying to hurry the car that would take her up to her office and away from any questions she couldn't answer.

Her heart thudding and her knees shaking, Ellen shut herself into her office and booted up her computer.

"Come on, come on," she muttered at it. As she waited, she checked her phone for missed calls or messages. Nothing. She surfed to the browser on her phone and checked the daily news.

Details were sketchy. A woman's body had been found on the street below Gabriel's apartment building. They didn't specify who found her or how she'd died, but they reported the death as suspicious. All the reports she checked mentioned police had taken in a person of interest for questioning but hadn't laid charges. None of the reports identified the woman or the suspect.

But the news was obviously out now, or the reporters wouldn't be downstairs in the lobby.

Frantic, Ellen tried Gabriel's cell phone, but as expected, it went to voicemail. She left a message for him to call her. She recalled Detective Morris's card and retrieved it from her wallet. He'd know something.

Fingers shaking, Ellen punched in his number. When she got only his voicemail, she burst into tears.

***

"Tell me again how Miss Weever ended up in your apartment." Detective Morris spoke in a conversational tone, but his expression showed suspicion and disbelief, and this was the third time he'd launched this question at Gabriel.

"I'll cover it as many times as you like, but the facts won't change," Gabriel said. "She was outside my building when I arrived home."

"In your car?"

"Walking—as I said the other two times I explained this to you." He gave a frustrated sigh, but he understood the exercise they did. No problem. His story wouldn't change because he stuck to facts. "She was drunk."

"You went with her to your place after the two of you went drinking?"

"No."

"Take it back a bit. Where were you coming home from?"

The interrogation room was cold and sparsely furnished. A metal table with a chair on each opposing side offered the only breaks from the tiled floor, and a two-way mirror adorned one of the puke-green brick walls.

Morris had given Gabriel water to drink, and he helped himself. They'd probably use it later to get his fingerprints and DNA, but he didn't care. At least they hadn't charged him with anything, which would be an alternative way of getting his prints.

He'd insisted on calling his lawyer, and they'd let him, but the lawyer wasn't in the room with him. If they charged Gabriel with anything later, he didn't want the lawyer to be disqualified from representing him, something Canadian law allowed. Gabriel told the man to call BRI to tell them what had happened so Ellen would know. He hoped she'd realize he'd had nothing to do with Katrina's death. Surely, she wouldn't assume ...

Please, Ellen, don't assume.

Gabriel sighed and started his story from the time he and Ellen had left the Italian restaurant. "She left in the rideshare, and I walked home. When I arrived at the front entrance to my apartment building, I found Katrina waiting for me, and she was plastered."

"This is where I'm fuzzy on the whole thing, Gabe. Can I call you Gabe?"

"No."

Morris frowned. "All right. Mr. Duncan. Tell me why you'd take an obviously sloshed woman into your apartment."

"I didn't want to send her home alone in a cab with a stranger in that condition. She was close to blackout drunk from the look of it. She'd be in danger. Who the hell knows what could've happened to her if I'd let her go home alone?"

"Look what happened to her when you didn't."

Gabriel scowled and the flush of rage flooded his face. "I didn't hurt her. She was safe with me, but I don't think she went over the balcony on her own." This was the first time he'd said his greatest fear out loud. Until now, he'd been too afraid to voice it. Anger had loosened his tongue, and Gabriel hoped he hadn't made a colossal error.

"Well, now, why would you say that?"

Gabriel ran a hand through his hair, mussing it up—

not that he'd had a chance to shower and make himself presentable before he'd called the cops. No, he'd seen Katrina down there and had immediately called 911. By the time the police arrived, he'd thrown on some clothes and brushed his teeth, but that was all.

"My apartment door was unlocked when I went to answer it to let the police in."

"You left it unlocked all night?"

"No. I locked it before I went to bed. Either Katrina unlocked it and let someone in, which means it was someone she knew, or someone broke in."

"You don't have a security system?"

"I didn't engage it. I didn't want Katrina to get up in the night and accidentally trigger it if she left." He'd regret that for the rest of his life. He should've just set the alarm and risked an accidental jolt out of bed when she—or whoever—opened the door.

"There's something else." He swallowed. "A trail led to the balustrade, but it wasn't distinct footprints. I avoided it when I went to look over the railing, so my path to and from the edge is distinct. Detective, the first trail is a mess, as if someone mussed it up to hide the footprints or as if someone dragged her out there. She wouldn't have jumped. Not her. And if she woke up and found herself in my apartment, why didn't she wake me? I half-expected her to try to climb into bed with me if she awoke in the night. That would've been more in character—she'd have at least tried. I even locked my bedroom door so she'd have to knock and wake me up if she wanted to talk to me."

Morris remained silent as Gabriel's words sank in. "Maybe, she tried. Maybe, you didn't like that so much and decided you wanted her out of your life permanently. Nothing you've said exonerates you. It could mean you planned this out."

"I planned this out? How? If I'd planned it out, I wouldn't have invited Ellen back to my place. The only reason she wasn't there when Katrina appeared is because it was Monday night, and she said she wanted to go home. I had no idea Katrina was out there waiting for me. Check the surveillance video, for Christ's sake. You'll see how it happened."

He went on the offensive. Enough of this bullshit. "Why aren't you doing that right now? Why aren't you getting evidence from my apartment? Cameras sit at every entrance on that building. Whoever was in my apartment would've been picked up coming and going." Unless whoever it was lived in the building, but what were the odds of that?

"Don't worry about the investigation, Mr. Duncan. We're getting all the evidence we need." He gave Gabriel a look that said whatever they got would verify he'd killed Katrina.

Gabriel decided he'd helped the investigation all he could, and it was time to go. He stood. "You gonna charge me with something? I've got work to do. If I think of anything else, I'll call you." Fake politeness dripped from every word, and an expression of unconcern settled on his face.

Morris also stood. "Don't leave town. I'll probably call you before you call me." His tone and expression left no doubt he meant it.

CHAPTER 18

Reporters clustered outside his apartment, and Gabriel avoided them by taking a rideshare to the office and having the driver drop him in the underground parking. From there, he used the elevator to go up to the third floor where the BRI offices were. Without stopping at his office, he went straight to Ellen's. The door was closed, and when he knocked, he heard nothing. He tried the door and found it locked. He almost turned away and left, but something told him to call out to her.

"Ellen? You in there?"

The door flew open within seconds.

When he saw her appearance, he took a step back, shocked at her red-rimmed eyes and tousled hair.

"Gabe. Oh, God."

Because she looked so unsteady on her feet and close to tears, he gently nudged her into the office and closed and locked the door behind them.

"They didn't charge me," he began, "and I came here as soon as they released me."

She didn't reply, just stared at him through huge, terrified eyes.

"I want to tell you what happened." He remembered her text from the night before, how happy and carefree it had sounded. He kept his voice gentle, as though dealing with a frightened puppy. "Can we sit? Talk? Will you do that for me?"

She nodded. Since the office was small, with just a desk, three chairs and a file cabinet, he guided her to the two chairs in front of her desk. She eased slowly into one, and he took the other.

Gabriel started talking immediately, keeping his voice low and calm. Bit by bit, he told her everything that had happened the night before from the moment he arrived at his apartment building to the moment he found Katrina's body down on the sidewalk. She listened without interrupting him, and he didn't know if that was a good sign. Her eyes remained large and terrified throughout his narration, her hands wringing and twisting in her lap.

"I called the police, and they questioned me for hours. Detective Morris suspected I threw her from the balcony, but he couldn't hold me. They have no proof I hurt her."

When he stopped talking, she spoke, head lowered, for the first time since that initial exclamation at the sight of him.

"I'm sorry all that happened to you," she whispered, her gaze riveted on her busy hands. "It must've been difficult to take her upstairs with you, but it was the responsible thing to do. I want to be angry about it, but I can't. I didn't like Katrina, but I wouldn't have left an inebriated woman alone on the sidewalk either. I wouldn't have even called her a cab." She turned her

115

wide-eyed gaze on him.

"Thank you for understanding."

She nodded, accepting the compliment. "I think if she hadn't died, we'd be having a different conversation."

"I did what my conscience told me to do, Ellen."

"You don't have to justify your actions to me. What she did makes me angry, but I can't confront her on it, now, can I?" She scrubbed her hands over her face and leaned back in her chair. "Doesn't matter. Gabe, what if she intended to let someone into your apartment all along?"

"I considered that," he said. He'd had a lot of time to consider every angle. "If that was the intent—if I was the target—why was she the one dead on the pavement and not me?"

"Oh, God." It came out on a moan. "Oh, God, it could've been you."

"If someone came into my apartment and killed her, why would they leave? Why not confront me?"

"Maybe they knew she was pass-out drunk and wanted to shut her up. This proves she was involved in whatever Fran had been up to."

"It proves nothing, but it raises a red flag. Katrina had nothing to do with keeping the books here even after you left, correct?"

"Correct. She was a programmer. But she had to submit her billable hours."

"Would she have inflated those numbers? Would you have noticed if she had?"

"She could've inflated them to a certain extent, but if she got greedy, I'd have noticed. After a while, you get used to seeing how much each software developer billed. They typically broke down into eighty percent working on development and twenty percent admin or other tasks, such as training or writing reports. They were adamant here that all employees filled in weekly reports providing a breakdown of what they considered billable versus non-billable hours even if the invoice went to an internal department."

"That makes sense. Do software developers have many business expenses?"

"Depends. Expenses might jump if the developer goes to a client's site, but typically, clients pay those expenses. However, if the 'client' is internal, then yes, BRI would pay the expenses."

"Can you investigate everything Katrina billed while she was here and see if there was any change after Fran started working here?" He paused. "Verify the date she left to go work elsewhere, too, and if the new company she works for has any connection to BRI."

"Okay." She remained in her seat, though, and she looked so grief-stricken he took her hands in his.

"I'm so sorry, Ellen. If I could do it over again—"

"You'd still take her into your apartment and give her a safe place to recover. If you were the type of guy who'd shove her in a cab with a stranger, I wouldn't want to be with you."

"You still do? You believe I didn't hurt her?"

"After all this time, I know you well enough to trust you didn't hurt her. You couldn't."

"I'm glad you think so because Morris might arrest me if they discover she was murdered, and I don't think she jumped off that balcony."

The grief and terror left her face, and she sat straight in her chair. "Then we have to prove you didn't do it."

***

117

"The first thing we need to do is go to your apartment and examine it," Ellen said.

"The police had it cordoned off. I'm not sure they'll let us in yet. I'll call Morris and tell him I need to go home. I could use a shower, anyway."

Ellen suggested he go to his office to call the detective while she checked the database for the hours Katrina had billed. But as soon as Gabriel left, Ellen's cell phone sounded, and the ringtone was Rhonda's.

Rhonda had obviously seen the news. "Hey, what the hell happened last night? I hear Gabe's been arrested."

"Not arrested. Questioned." Ellen went to her desk and dug a chocolate bar from her stash. As she talked to Rhonda, she broke off small pieces and ate them as quietly as she could. It didn't fool her friend.

"You stress eating?"

"I'm stress snacking. It's not the same. Just some chocolate."

"Gabe will be okay, right? He didn't do it?"

"No, he didn't, but I want to ask you if Max would help him if they charge him."

"Max is a prosecutor. He can't help."

"Damn. Well, would he advise us? From the perspective of the opposition? Gabe is innocent. They shouldn't charge him, but if they do, we'll need help."

"We? What's this 'we' business?"

"I'm sticking by him no matter what. He didn't do it. I won't let them put him in jail for something he didn't do."

"You sound awfully certain. Were you there?"

Ellen hesitated. "No. But I know him."

"Are you sure your relationship with him hasn't

clouded your judgment? It looks bad. From an objective perspective, I mean."

"What are you saying? You don't believe me when I tell you he's innocent?"

"Don't get excited. I'm not sure he did it, but I'm also not sure he didn't do it. What if he killed those two women? He's a link to them both, isn't he?"

Ellen had no answer to that, so she returned to her original question. "If I need legal advice, can I trust Max to give it to me?"

Wariness in her voice, Rhonda said, "Why do you need legal advice?"

"If the police don't find the real killer, we have to. If I need help, I want to know you have my back."

"I have your back, Ellen. I'll always have your back. But if he's guilty, you're putting yourself in danger by helping him. If you find proof he did it, you could end up like Fran and Katrina."

Ellen gasped, unable to believe what her friend— her best friend—was saying. Through gritted teeth, she said, "I'm not in any danger. Gabe would never hurt me."

She knew that was true. All she had to do was prove it to the world.

CHAPTER 19

Detective Morris gave Gabriel the go-ahead to return home, and after spending an hour with Ellen reviewing Katrina's billable hours, the date she'd left the company and where she'd gone, and her new employer's relationship to BRI, the two left the office and took a rideshare to Gabriel's building. Katrina's billable hours had increased by a third about two months after Francesca started at BRI, she'd remained with the company until the spring—the approximate time Gabriel showed interest in purchasing BRI—and the company she moved to had no connection to her former workplace.

No reporters hovered outside the apartment complex when Gabriel and Ellen arrived. Even so, they directed the driver to take the vehicle into the underground parking and went to Gabriel's apartment unit from there.

When they entered his home, the first thing Gabriel noticed was the mess the police had left from their evidence-gathering. Fingerprint powder dusted surfaces. Furniture had shifted. He made a mental note to call a cleaning service and send the bill to the police department.

The second thing he noticed was that Katrina's coat, purse, and shoes were gone. He assumed the police had removed them and kicked himself for not thinking to go through the coat's pockets and the purse's contents the night before. But why would he? He'd had no inkling anything tragic would happen to her while he slept, and after he found her body, shock muddled his thinking. So, if she had a cell phone on her, he hadn't noticed. It'd likely been in her purse or coat pocket, but now, he'd never know.

Unless it's entered as evidence against me, and I get to see it during the discovery phase of my trial. Whatever that meant. He'd heard it on television. *Stop it. You didn't do it. They won't charge you.* But the fear and anxiety they would do just that lingered. He hoped it wouldn't give him an ulcer before they caught the true killer.

He took Ellen's coat and hung it up in the coat closet in the foyer, and she set her purse on the floor inside the same closet.

"I don't want to touch too much until we go through it," she explained.

"The police would've taken any evidence." He pointed at the white carpet where the ceramic floor ended. "Looks like a shoe print there."

They crouched down and examined it. Gabriel snapped a picture with his phone. "I removed my shoes when I brought her inside."

When Ellen frowned at him, he said, "I remember because I had to toe them off while I held on to Katrina. It wasn't easy. She was dead weight."

"But you still thought of taking off your shoes

before you stepped on the carpet."

"I didn't know she'd be killed!"

"I wasn't calling you self-centred," she replied. "If I owned carpet this white, I'd have done the same thing. Couldn't have been good for the shoes."

"The shoes are easier to clean." He shook his head. "That isn't my shoe print."

"Could be the cops," she suggested.

"They all wore booties when they entered the apartment. I noticed." It wasn't out of courtesy, either, but so they wouldn't contaminate any evidence. He didn't tell Ellen that, but based on her woebegone expression, she understood the implications.

"Besides, I was still in here when one of them huddled around this spot with a camera and measuring tape. They flagged and taped around it, but I guess they removed those when they left."

When she continued to look stricken, he tried to console her. "That's a good thing. They'll check my shoes against this and verify it's not mine."

"Sure," she agreed, "but they might've missed something. We should look around. You know your place best. You can tell if something's missing."

"Do you think the fact that the police didn't walk me through to do the same means they're focused on me as a suspect?"

"I hope not. Maybe they were looking at it as a suicide." She whirled to face him then, and throwing her arms around him, she buried her face in his shoulder. "We can't let them arrest you. We'll figure this out."

He returned the hug and pressed his face into her hair. It smelled like flowers, and he inhaled deeply, allowing the scent to soothe his frayed nerves. He and

Ellen had just reconnected. How could everything have gone so wrong? Did all this result from his purchase of BRI? He'd had people review the financials. No one had red-flagged anything other than to say their business practices were wasteful. He tried to recall who'd been involved in that. Francesca had helped. She'd provided the information required for the evaluation.

"She hid it when I examined their books," he said.

Ellen raised her head, and he was relieved to see her eyes were dry. He couldn't have her falling apart on him. He needed her too much, not only emotionally and as a comforting physical presence but also to help him find out who was framing him. What if this murder was deliberately done at his apartment? Someone had seen the opportunity in Katrina's presence here and seized it. Who else but Gabriel would the cops suspect?

"Hid what?" Ellen asked, drawing him from his musings and tilting her head up to meet his gaze.

"What they were doing. The monkey business. Fran had control over which files we accessed when we did our due diligence on the company before I bought it. Maybe she thought she could carry on doing it after I bought it, but then I fired her." He released Ellen and she took a step backward.

"Gabe." Her voice relayed she'd thought of something that had frightened her. "If Katrina had a hand in this, she might've killed Fran when she learned you'd let Fran go, but if she didn't kill herself, then someone else was also involved." She shook her head, negating that theory. "But by the time you bought BRI, Katrina had moved on. Why would she do that if she was successfully stealing from the company with Fran's help?"

He shrugged. "Maybe she wanted to move on before I bought the place and found them out."

"Fran would've stayed if you hadn't let her go, and she would've continued to skim."

"I might've found out."

Ellen shook her head. "Not if she was careful and you trusted her."

He started walking around the apartment, Ellen tailing him.

"I'd have trusted her, you know," he said.

"I know."

After they examined the sofa where Katrina had slept and the chair where her belongings had sat, Ellen wandered to the balcony doors. She stood in front of the glass as if wrestling with whether to slide them open. Gabriel strode over to stand beside her.

"Might as well look." He opened them, noting as he did that the police had left them unlocked. *Doesn't matter. With all the cops in and out, no one would dare come in this way—not today, at any rate.* But when they left, he'd make sure to engage the alarm.

Before she could step outside, Gabriel blocked Ellen with an arm across her chest. "Wait. Let me scope it out first."

She made no comment but remained inside.

He took one step onto the balcony and scanned the small, empty area. All his patio furniture was down in the storage room. Any potted plants he kept outside in the summer he'd brought inside for the winter. Not much to see at all. Even the tracks he'd found in the early morning cold had melted into mush. No protective awning or upper balcony existed to block the elements. A slight overhang allowed him to step outside in stocking feet, but water and slushy snow covered almost the entire remaining area.

Ellen's voice broke the silence. "Is it horrible that I want to go look over the side?"

"You won't see anything."

When she didn't respond, he turned to face her and discovered she'd gone back to get her boots. When she appeared with them in her hand, he stepped aside.

"I need to see how far down ..." She gulped and couldn't finish her thought, and she wore a grief-stricken expression.

"Why?" Maybe it *was* horrible she wanted to look over the side. He'd avoided answering her question because he didn't have an answer. Was it morbid curiosity that led her to do so or some misguided attempt at empathy for the dead woman?

Ellen slipped on her boots and tiptoed to the balustrade. When she reached it, she paused a moment and then peered over the top.

"Railing's pretty high."

He waited, letting her work through whatever she needed to, to process what had happened. That might explain why she wanted to see the site where Katrina's body had landed.

"Do you think that means a man did it? You'd have to be strong to throw someone off the balcony." She looked back at him, her brows lifted questioningly. "Wouldn't you?"

"Or a strong woman."

"Do you think she fought?"

He considered the question. "I would've heard that."

"And yet, you didn't. How could she still be unconscious? I know you said she was blackout drunk, but was she so bad she didn't wake up when someone picked her up and carried her outside to throw her from the balcony?"

She shook her head emphatically from side to side. "How? Why? Who could do this?" Tears sprang to her eyes. "I can't understand this." Hysteria laced her voice.

"Ellen, come away from there."

She placed a hand gently on top of the railing. "I'm so sorry," she whispered. She raised her head and met his gaze. "I was jealous, Gabe. I didn't want her in your life, but that doesn't mean I wished her dead. Do you think? I didn't wish her dead."

Did she actually think her thoughts had somehow manifested Katrina's death? He started to go to her, sock feet and slush pile be damned, when she rushed into his arms, sobbing.

"All right." He eased her back inside, slid the door closed, and, after helping her remove her boots, walked her to the couch. "Of course you didn't. Whoever killed her did it for their own sick reasons, and if we can figure that out, we might find out who it was. But you had nothing to do with this." He wanted to tell her how silly that line of thinking was but didn't. It wouldn't help anything. No one liked to be told they were ridiculous.

She quieted, and when she had herself under control again, she stood. "Let's keep searching, then. We have to find out who did this. I can't stop thinking about how it must have felt for her." She shuddered.

"Okay, let's check my room next. I'm sure we won't find anything there. She was never in my room."

Gabriel led Ellen into the bedroom. His bed remained unmade, and his pyjamas and slippers lay strewn about the floor. In the en suite bathroom, nothing appeared out of place. He'd used the toilet and then the toothbrush and toothpaste but had touched nothing else, to his recollection. His comb, maybe, but it sat in its place in the cabinet.

"If anyone came into my room, it was while I was sleeping, and I never woke up to notice. By the time the sound woke me, they'd left. Except they couldn't have entered my room while I slept," he added. "I'd locked the bedroom door. They'd have had to bust in."

"They couldn't have hidden in the apartment and waited for you to leave? Or left while you were on the balcony?"

He thought about it. Took himself back to 3:00 in the morning and his disorientation upon awakening. "A noise woke me. I'd had a dream, but I can't remember it." He concentrated, trying to recall the dream, the sounds in it. *Whoosh*. He replayed it in his mind. Yes, that would've been the balcony doors. He'd heard no scream, no apartment door slamming, no voice ...

"Cat got your tongue," he said.

"What?" Ellen frowned, puzzled.

"Let's return to the living room."

He strode from the en suite and through the bedroom, discarding any notion that the voice he'd heard had come from inside his room. His door had been closed and locked, and when he'd left the room this morning, he'd had to unlock and open it.

Rolling drum. His door had been shut tight, and the sound hadn't been someone knocking on his bedroom door or even attempting to open it. No, not rolling. Dragging.

"Loud enough to wake me," he said.

"What?"

"The sound." He walked through his living room, through his dining room, his den, his office, his guest room, the en suite bath off the guest room, the powder room, the kitchen ...

"Nothing. Not a damn thing that would make that sound." Frustrated, he retraced his steps to the apartment's door, opened it, and let it slam closed. It banged shut, reverberating through the apartment. "He wouldn't have slammed the door behind him," Gabriel stated. "That would've been stupid."

"Why are you obsessing about this?" Ellen asked.

"Because he threw Katrina off the balcony and did something in my home that woke me up. What the hell did he do?" A horrible, creeping sensation up his spine stopped him in his tracks. He stared at the chairs around the dining room table. One sat pushed back three centimetres from the table though all seven of the others snugged up against it. He gazed up at the crystal chandelier dangling above the dark cherry wood table. His eyes widened, and he gripped Ellen's arm. Holding a finger up to his lips to signal her to silence, he guided her back out into the hallway.

When the door closed behind them, he said, "I know what woke me, and I know what made the noise I heard."

CHAPTER 20

"What is it?" Ellen whispered, afraid if she spoke too loudly this nightmare would indeed be real.

"A listening device. In my chandelier."

She must've looked at him as if he'd lost his mind because he said, "Someone dragged the chair away from the table, which I heard. Why else climb up there except to put something on my light fixture?"

"The police could've moved it."

"Sure," he replied, "but you're forgetting the sound. I heard someone dragging the chair along the floor. The guy probably had shoes on too." Gabriel scowled. "Let's check."

"You going to search for the device?"

"I have to. If I show it to Morris, it'll show I didn't kill Katrina." His expression grew thoughtful, and he said, "I'm not sure I'd want to tell him yet though."

"We have to. He should know what's going on. At least, you need to rule out the police put it there." She'd grown tired of playing detective. They needed to let the professionals take over. Gabriel seemed to be enjoying this way too much, but she had no desire to play amateur sleuth. "Whatever's going on, let the police handle it, especially if you're bugged."

"The police only started investigating me this morning, and they'd have to go through legal channels to allow them to do place a bug. Let's prove first it's there." He led her back into the apartment and to the dining chair in question. He covered his hands with his shirtsleeves and dragged the chair away from the table. Bending close to the padded seat, he examined it for a moment before he stood up again. Silently, he pointed to a faint grey scuff on the cushion.

In his stocking feet, he climbed on the chair and searched the light fixture. After a few minutes, his gaze met Ellen's, and he signalled her a thumbs-up.

He'd located the listening device.

Oh my God. What if the killer heard something to make him think we're onto him? He'll come after us. She didn't say any of that aloud but turned an expression of agony to Gabriel.

***

Two hours later, Ellen and Gabriel sat in the chairs before Detective Morris's desk in his office. Morris leaned against the desk in front of them, his posture casual, his expression bemused.

"Say again? You found a what?"

"A listening device. Hidden in the chandelier above my dining table."

"Why? What could anyone possibly want to listen to in your apartment?"

Not sure if she should be offended on Gabriel's behalf at Morris's question, Ellen asked, "Did your people put it there, Detective?" As Gabriel had said before, it wasn't likely, but she wanted to verify. If Morris had ordered it installed, he'd have to come clean about it, wouldn't he?

"Of course not. Would be a drastic move." He crossed his arms and levelled his gaze on Gabriel. "You colluding in these murders, Duncan?"

"No," Gabriel said. "If I was, and if I thought the listening device belonged to you, we wouldn't be here telling you about it."

Morris's arms dropped to his side, and his shoulders relaxed. "Even so, I don't get the entire connection to you. You're hiding something from me." He first met Gabriel's gaze and then fixed on Ellen's. "Both of you."

"We have to tell him what we know, Gabe," Ellen said, wincing at the annoyed expression he threw her way. "I know you don't want to, but if we don't, you or I could be next." If they revealed what they suspected to Morris, he'd find the real killer, and they'd be safe and could get on with their lives.

Gabriel still looked dubious, and his lips pressed firmly together as though he would refuse to speak.

"What exactly do you know?" Morris asked.

Ellen opened her mouth to reply, but Gabriel interjected. "It's all speculation. We don't have any proof. That's why we haven't said anything to you."

Morris gave an audible sigh of frustration. "Any little thing can help this investigation, Mr. Duncan. Tell me what you know, and let me decide what's a clue. That's my job."

Gabriel talked then and gave Morris everything they knew or suspected: the link between Katrina and Francesca; the possibility one or both women had been bilking BRI; the suspicion that someone else was involved; and the fear that whoever their accomplice was, he wasn't done with his crimes. Ellen lent supporting statements whenever she spotted the opportunity to clarify or corroborate what Gabriel said.

"If either woman was about to expose him or cause him to be exposed, it would give him motive to kill them," Gabriel concluded.

"Going into your apartment with you in it was rather a bold step, don't you think?" Morris asked. Before Gabriel could respond, he added, "I'm not saying he didn't. Or she. I'm not ruling out it's a woman. But whoever went into your apartment to plant the bug and kill Miss Weever took a huge risk to do it."

"Maybe he didn't intend to do it that way," Ellen said. "No one expected Katrina to be there that night. As Gabe said, I could've been there with him had I accepted his invitation to return to his apartment. I suppose I could've escorted her home then, but I'm not sure that's what we'd have decided to do."

"What didn't happen isn't my concern here. We need to examine what did happen," Morris replied. "But I get your point. The killer might've feared Katrina had already revealed everything, and he planted the bug to find out. It's possible she let him into the apartment herself. We saw no evidence of a break-in at the unit."

"What do we do now?" Ellen asked. "If we remove the bug, whoever planted it will know we've discovered it. If we keep it, he can listen in to everything that goes on in Gabe's unit. No one wants to restrict everything they do and say in their own home."

"We'll remove it," Morris replied. "Try to trace it to

the owner. We'll examine the dining room chair for prints as well. I'll set that up right now."

Gabe agreed to meet the team at his apartment, and he and Ellen left the police station. They walked the short distance to where Gabriel had parked his car and got in.

"I'm dropping you at the office," Gabriel said. "Keep digging in those files. We need to, now more than ever. I'll meet with the cops at my apartment and then catch up to you before you leave the office."

"All right." She waited, suspecting he wanted to say more.

"Can we have dinner again tonight?"

She hesitated but reconsidered when she remembered Katrina had gained entry to Gabriel's apartment because Ellen had refused to return there with him. *Will I have to spend every waking moment with him in case someone else ambushes him?*

"Maybe you shouldn't go to your apartment by yourself."

"I have to. We've both got work to do. It'll be fine. The police will meet me there. What could happen?"

"You ask me? Anything," she replied, worry dripping from every word.

"I'll be careful."

"Why don't you come to my place after work?" She almost retracted the invitation as soon as it was out. Her parents, especially her mother, would grill him more than Detective Morris ever could. But they'd be safe at her place. Four adults in the house would deter any intrusion.

He agreed, and though Ellen didn't approve, he drove her to the office and then continued on to his apartment.

CHAPTER 21

As Ellen expected, her parents descended on her and Gabriel the moment the two stepped in the door. Joanne invited them to come upstairs to have dinner, but Ellen declined the invitation, suggesting they do it another time. Gabriel offered to take them all out for dinner on Sunday, to Joanne's delight and Ellen's chagrin. They hung their coats up on hooks at the top of the stairs, and Ellen ushered Gabriel down to her lair. When she'd led him to safety in her basement apartment, she started to apologize for her parents' intrusiveness, but he brushed it off.

"They seem like nice people. Down to earth."

"Down to earth? No. Anything but. My mother is more out of this world than down to earth."

"Cute. I look forward to getting to know them better."

"All right. But remember, you asked for it."

He waved an arm around the living room where they stood, encompassing the padded sectional sofa, gas fireplace, and big-screen television. "Looks comfortable."

"It is. But I want to make it as temporary as possible." The reason for her need to live here intruded into her mind then, almost making her regret the decision to invite him in. Best she make dinner quickly and send him on his way.

She offered him a drink, and he accepted a glass of red wine. She poured them both a glass, and they toasted and sipped. When she set her glass down on the kitchen island and told him to make himself comfortable, he removed his suit jacket, rolled up his sleeves, and asked her what she wanted him to do to help.

Ellen raised her brows. "You cook?"

"Yes, ma'am. When I was a boy, I hung out in the kitchen with the cook all the time."

"You had a cook?"

In all the time she'd known him, he'd never talked about his family. His father was always in the news since he owned a billion-dollar software company, but she'd heard nothing about his mother. At least, she didn't recall hearing anything about his mother.

"Yes. My mother died when I was young—ten. Even before my mother died, I spent most of my time hanging out in the kitchen and considered becoming a chef at one time. I took some courses and tried to pursue it. Somehow, I ended up working in my father's company instead. It's what he always wanted for me."

"What about what you wanted?" Ellen pulled some vegetables from the crisper and set them on the counter beside the sink. "The cutting board is underneath on the left. Knives are in a wooden block in the cupboard, top right. You wash and chop. I'll get some pasta going."

"I don't know what happened to what I wanted. Somehow, it became less important even to me. Working for my father was always interesting, and it kept me busy. It's not like I had an aversion to business, and the degree I got in it is useful. Makes me a lot of money."

The word "money" hung in the air between them, making Ellen think about the money Francesca, and, perhaps, Katrina, had stolen. Was it just for themselves, or had they stuck their necks out for someone else? This mysterious killer-slash-partner who pulled their strings? Surely, it couldn't be someone still at BRI.

She turned her attention back to the work at hand, tabling for the time being her ponderings about the killer. They worked amicably together on a pasta primavera. Ellen sliced up a loaf of Italian bread and made garlic bread while Gabriel tossed together a quick Caesar salad. She poured them each a second glass of wine when they sat side by side on barstools at the island to eat.

"To better days," Ellen said, raising her glass.

"Cheers," Gabriel replied.

***

After dinner, Gabriel helped Ellen clean up the dishes, and the mood lightened further as they laughed and chatted about anything other than work. With the kitchen cleaned up, Ellen asked Gabriel if he'd like coffee and dessert.

"Dessert? What did you have in mind?" He wiggled his brows at her as she closed the dishwasher and turned to face him, almost bumping into him as she did.

He gripped her upper arms to steady her, and she laughed nervously. Her mind instantly set to wondering if she'd allow the evening to turn into something more than a friendly dinner. Her body flashed back to their one night together, and electric heat raced to her core.

Without thinking, she threw her arms around him and pulled his head down so their lips met. As before, her lips grew demanding, telling him in no uncertain terms where she wanted this to go.

He exhaled a soft breath, parted her lips with his tongue, and explored her with his hands. When she tried to break away, he yanked her in tighter, but she pressed on his shoulders, and he gave her the space she requested.

On a gasp of air, she said, "The bedroom. That way." She pointed in its general direction, trusting he'd take the not-so-subtle hint, and he did.

Ever the efficiency expert, he removed his tie, his shirt, and his pants as he rushed for the bedroom door. Laughingly, she followed his example, and they left a trail of discarded clothing in their wake. By the time they reached the bed, both were naked, and, as before, Ellen appreciated what he offered her.

His body, lean and defined, reminded her of a perfectly sculpted statue. The sight of it made her crave to run her hands all over it, to explore every inch. She had to have him or she'd lose her mind. She darted past him and ripped the covers back, but before the insanity of lust took over completely, she pulled open the drawer in her nightstand and handed him a condom.

"You're gonna need this."

He accepted it, ripping it frantically from her hand,

tearing it open, and rolling it on. Practical matters out of the way, he grabbed her, and together, they dropped onto the bed. Instantly, their bodies pressed together though he had yet to penetrate her. His kisses covered her face, her throat. She tilted her head back so her neck arched into his lips. His hands fluttered over her hips, her abdomen, and higher until one hand palmed her breast. Once he'd captured it, she gasped, writhing under him as her loins caught the fire of need.

"I can't wait," she cried out. "Please." The ache inside her became unbearable.

He raised his head to meet her gaze, and she recognized the same impassioned torture in his expression that spurred her own desperate need for him to fill her.

"Please," she begged. "Please." She whispered it over and over, each time growing hungrier with desire. To encourage him, to draw him into her, she opened her thighs, ready to receive him, and gripped his cock with her hand to guide him.

He slid in easily, and she cried out in triumph as he moved inside her. She met him thrust for thrust, both of them racing toward a peak only the other could provide. When release finally came, Ellen cried out from the unbearable pleasure.

CHAPTER 22

It took Gabriel a while to catch his breath after their initial exertion, but when he did, he made love to Ellen more slowly, savouring every touch, every taste, every caress—both the ones he received and the ones he gave. They didn't discuss if he should stay; they both knew he would, and both wanted him to.

He peeked at her clock radio after she'd drifted off, nestled in the crook of his arm, and, to his amazement, it was only eleven o'clock. Though she probably thought he'd expected their night to end this way, he hadn't. He'd assumed she'd want to wait indefinitely before allowing their relationship to get physical again. That she trusted him enough to get this close so quickly gave him hope that, this time, things would work out for them.

From the hallway came the sound of a text message arriving. At first, he was tempted to ignore it but reconsidered. It was likely his phone—Ellen's was probably still in her purse. His phone was in his pants pocket, and the pants lay on the floor; he should probably pick them up so the phone didn't get stepped on.

He slipped out of bed and left the bedroom. He picked his way through the trail of discarded clothing, slipping on his briefs the moment he found them. When he located his pants, he fished in the pocket for his phone and checked the display. A text from Carl.

That night from a year ago came flooding back, and rage bubbled up inside. He forced it down with a deep breath and a reminder that, this time, Carl had no idea Gabriel was with Ellen. He needn't assume this was bad news. He logged into his phone and opened the message: Fran's husband called me. He wants to meet with us. May I set it up?

Gabriel replied: He called you now?

The response took only a moment: Yes. He's upset.

The conversation was getting frustrating, so Gabriel texted: Can I call you now?

When Carl responded in the affirmative, Gabriel phoned his friend.

"Why are you up?" Carl said the moment he answered the call.

"I just am." No reason to divulge where he was. Gabriel closed Ellen's bedroom door so he wouldn't disturb her and went into the kitchen, the room farthest from the bedroom.

"So, are you available to meet with Zach Newton tomorrow night?"

"Yeah. Where?"

"I'll make it a coffee shop. Don't want this to involve alcohol."

"Does he have an alcohol problem?"

"Not that I know of."

"Why does he want to meet with us? How do you

even know him?"

"I met him a few times. BRI functions. He came to the company Christmas party with Fran. They invited clients and contractors too, so I went. We hit it off, and I went golfing with him a few times."

Interesting. Gabriel hunted for a glass in Ellen's cupboard, and when he found one, he got himself water from the cooler next to the fridge. "Is this the first time since Fran died that he's called you?"

"First time he called me, but I called him to give him my condolences when I heard she'd passed away."

"How'd that conversation go?"

"About how you'd expect. He was devastated. This came out of the blue, you know? He said she seemed happy even though she'd lost her job. Sure, she was worried about how long it'd take her to get another one, but he said she assured him she had enough contacts that she'd get work quickly."

"She say who these contacts were?"

"I didn't grill him about it, Gabe. He was hurting. I told him how sorry I was and said if he ever needed anything to call me. I guess he needs something."

Yes, but what? And why from me? "Did he say why he wants to meet with us?"

"He thinks she didn't kill herself and wanted to talk about it with me."

Stunned, Gabriel said, "Did he ask to talk to me?"

"No. I suggested it. I don't know what the hell she got messed up in if her husband thinks she was murdered, but I'd bet it relates to Katrina's death. I figured you'd want to hear whatever he had to say."

"You thought right. Listen, one more thing while I've got you." He glanced toward Ellen's room and shivered as he suddenly remembered he was nearly naked. An afghan lay spread across the back of the sofa, and Gabriel snatched it up and draped it around his shoulders.

"Yeah?"

"You told Ellen Fran wanted to meet with you."

"She told you?" Carl didn't sound angry, but he didn't sound pleased either. More like irritated.

That he'd get annoyed with Ellen for discussing this with her boyfriend, a man who had a vested interest in having this information, had Gabriel frowning. When he replied, his tone was sharp. "I needed to know."

"You did. But not from her."

"She's my—we're working on this together, and I'm your best friend." Something Gabriel questioned at times; though, in two decades of friendship, they'd never come this close to having their loyalties to each other tested.

"Yeah, and I would've told you."

"We've talked since then, and you never mentioned it." Gabriel dropped onto the couch, tucking his legs up under the afghan.

"I never got a chance. Look, I'm getting you a meetup with Zach. And before you ask, I have no idea why Fran wanted to meet. She never said. For all I know, it had nothing to do with what led to her death."

"Did Zach know she wanted to meet with you?"

The phone fell silent as Carl contemplated. "I got the impression we'd be meeting behind his back but not to start an affair or anything."

"She gave no hint about what she wanted to discuss?"

"She knew you and I are friends. Maybe she wanted to talk about you. She might've thought I could get you to hire her back. All I can do is guess. If she wanted me to do something like that, she never said."

"Okay, thanks, Carl. I'd better go. Text me with the details when you set up the meeting."

"Will do."

They said their goodbyes and disconnected the call.

The soft rattle of the doorknob turning on Ellen's bedroom door made him look in that direction. Ellen, wearing a robe, stood in the doorway, her face white, her expression terrified.

As soon as she saw him, her shoulders dropped and her face relaxed. She scrubbed her hands across her face and, with a visible sigh, walked over to where he sat.

"What's going on?" Though her posture had shown her relief at finding him still in the house, her tone betrayed worry.

"That was Carl," he replied.

"Walker?"

"Yeah. Sorry if I woke you."

She gave him a rueful smile. "I woke up and found you gone. I guess I panicked."

Not panicked. She was terrified I'd walked out on her again. He couldn't blame her. Nothing had gone right for them after they'd slept together that fateful night.

He took his glass to the sink and strode over to stand before her. Taking her in his arms, he buried his face in her soft, fragrant hair. Neither spoke for a moment; both revelled in the other's touch, the other's presence.

Without lifting his face from her hair, he said, "It'll never happen again, Ellen. Nothing will make me leave you."

"Did he say something about me?" She sounded taken aback.

"No, not at all," he said quickly. "He wanted to set up a meeting."

She moved her head, forcing his chin up, and angled her face so their gazes met. "He wanted to set up a meeting at eleven o'clock at night?"

"Sit down and I'll explain."

CHAPTER 23

"I want to go too," Ellen said as soon as Gabriel finished telling her about his conversation with Carl. "You can't go alone."

"I won't be alone. Carl will be with me."

"What if Carl killed Fran? What if this is a trap?" For all she knew, Carl had started the rumour about her supposed engagement. They had only his word that a woman had told him about it.

Gabriel shook his head, scowling. "Not Carl. No way. I've known him for years. He's not capable of murder."

"Are you sure?" She whispered it, afraid to say it too loud and either make it true or make Gabriel angry.

"Positive." He stroked her hair and pulled her closer to him on the couch where they sat.

"Don't worry. I'll be fine. As soon as we're done at the coffee shop, I'll call you."

She had no choice but to agree. "Okay. Let's go back to bed."

He gave her no argument over that, and they

returned to her bed but not to sleep.

***

The next night after work, Ellen walked to Foundation to meet up with Rhonda. She'd called her friend during the day and asked to meet for drinks, and Rhonda had agreed. This would keep Ellen distracted until she heard from Gabriel that all was well.

Surprisingly, Rhonda wasn't alone when she walked up to the booth where Ellen sat sipping a glass of red wine; Max and John accompanied her.

They all exchanged greetings and took seats on the benches, John snagging a place next to Ellen.

"Hope you don't mind the guys joining us," Rhonda said. "Max called me this afternoon, and I invited them along."

Ellen smiled. "No, it's fine."

What else could she say? And it *was* fine. Max and Rhonda were officially together now, and John wasn't bad company—as long as he understood nothing would happen between them. She'd just have to lead the conversation around to her new relationship somehow.

"How are things at work?" John asked Ellen after the server had taken their drink orders.

"Busy. I've got a lot to do that'll keep me occupied for at least the next few weeks. How about you?"

He shrugged. "Always a full caseload. How are things with the BRI takeover?"

"Fine. Everything should get on track with Gabriel Duncan helping the company now." She saw her opening and grabbed it. "It was nice to reconnect with him. We've started dating." She glanced at John in her periphery. His expression remained neutral.

"I thought you should know," she added.

"I appreciate you wanted to inform me, but we weren't dating, as you so frequently remind me. I was just your beard for your mom's party."

She thought she detected a twinge of hurt in his voice, and guilt washed over her, but she shrugged it off. She'd been open with him about where they stood right from the start. "I'm glad you understand."

Their drinks appeared, and she picked up her glass of red wine and saluted. "To good friends."

The others raised their glasses. "To good friends."

***

At a coffee shop in the Eaton Centre, Gabriel sipped on a latte and watched the entrance for any sign of Carl or Zach. From where he sat, he could see both Dundas Street and Yonge Street. The moment Carl and Zach appeared, he'd spot them.

He checked the time again. They were five minutes late. Could this be some kind of ploy to get him to sit here while they ... He could think of no way to end that statement. Besides, Carl was his best friend. He'd never do anything to hurt Gabriel. Ellen's voice intruded on his thoughts, asking if Carl could be the killer.

Never. But Zach could.

Two men strolling along Yonge Street caught Gabriel's eye then. Carl and Zach approached the coffee shop together, deep in some serious conversation, based on their facial expressions. When they entered the café, Carl spotted Gabriel first and waved to him. The two men approached the counter and placed their orders. Carl paid for both, and they approached the table, their expressions sober.

Gabriel matched their mood. The conversation they were about to have could cause Zach grief. Carl knew nothing of Ellen's investigation into Francesca's suspicious activities, and Gabriel wasn't sure how much he should reveal to her husband. What if he'd been in on it? Somehow, the man didn't come across as a wife-killer, especially if the wife was responsible for most of their income—and Gabriel assumed she'd been the one making the big bucks. Zach was a sales clerk at a shoe store. He probably topped up his base salary with commissions but not to the extent that allowed them to live the lifestyle they had. That had to be all Francesca and her ill-gotten gains.

After exchanging greetings, Gabriel sat back and sipped his coffee, letting Carl take the lead. He got right to it.

"Zach asked me to help him figure out what happened to Francesca. The police haven't given him anything though they grilled him extensively the day after she died. We thought maybe you could shed some light on her final days at work," Carl said.

"I looked at her attendance record, the billable hours she tracked. She showed up every day, except for the odd day off here and there, until BRI packaged her out. Nothing in her HR files or in her billing reports suggest she had any physical or mental health issues," Gabriel replied. That was all accurate and something he could tell the dead woman's husband without revealing anything about her shady activities. But he didn't come to this meeting solely to reassure the grieving man. He too wanted information.

Keeping his gaze trained on Zach and studying the other man's face for any nuance of expression, Gabriel asked, "How were things at home?" Might as well be direct, try to catch Francesca's husband off guard.

"Fine. Nothing out of the ordinary." Zach's brows furrowed, and his mouth turned down, his expression veering more toward anguish than anything else.

"What do you think happened, then?"

"Christ, I think she was doing something behind my back." Zach buried his face in his hands a moment, but when he looked up again, his eyes were dry. He leaned back in his seat, one arm stretched out and retaining contact with the handle on his coffee mug. His other hand rested in his lap. "I think whatever it was got her killed." The worry in his expression was clear, but was it worry his own involvement would be revealed? This could all be an act to make Gabriel think whatever Francesca did at work had nothing to do with her husband.

Gabriel decided to play dumb. "You mean an affair?"

"No!" Zach's rage at the suggestion appeared genuine, but so had his worry and grief. Either the guy's performance was Oscar-worthy, or he actually had no idea what his wife had been up to.

"Then what?" Gabriel pressed.

"I think she was involved in something illegal." He now had the harried look of a man plagued by doubt and strain.

"Without your knowledge?" Gabriel's tone indicated he doubted the possibility.

"I thought she wanted to climb the corporate ladder. Succeed in her job and get to the top of her industry."

When Zach stopped talking and didn't seem to want to continue, Gabriel nudged him. "What do you think now?"

"I think I shouldn't be telling you this."

"You came here to do that, though, didn't you? Otherwise, why agree to meet me?"

"I need to get out from under this. You don't understand. If she made money illegally, I've got it now."

"Do you?"

He shrugged. "I don't know. If she has a windfall somewhere, she hid it so I can't even find it. But it has to be coming from somewhere." He leaned forward, and his voice dropped conspiratorially. "Our bills continue to be paid, and I don't know where the money's coming from. Get it? Someone might know about this, and whoever killed her might come looking for it. Or the police might discover what she was up to and think I was in on it." He glanced at Carl before returning his attention to Gabriel. "Carl told me you're going over the accounts at BRI. Maybe you can find out if that's where the money's coming from."

Gabriel stared daggers at Carl. They'd have to have a private chat later about what was okay to reveal to a dead woman's husband. In the meantime, Zach awaited a response, and Gabriel didn't know what to tell him or how. But he'd have to say something because whatever Francesca had been up to could now get all of them killed.

CHAPTER 24

For Ellen, the night crawled by, becoming more interminable the longer she heard nothing from Gabriel. Twice, she contemplated texting him but didn't. If he was still in the meeting, she didn't want him to think she was checking up out of worry even though that's exactly what she'd be doing. Her companions appeared oblivious to her distraction.

Rhonda and Max obviously had a deep rapport. They spent a lot of time gazing into each other's eyes, finishing each other's sentences, and sharing bites from each other's plates. Ellen ordered her usual stress food of chicken wings and fries, while John ordered a burger and fries. Neither offered the other a taste of anything, and rather than finishing each other's sentences, they carried on a halting and forced conversation about nothing.

John kept bringing the subject back to work, hers and his, and Ellen concluded this was the subject area in which he felt most comfortable. But that's the area she strictly wanted to avoid, especially as it related to the murder investigations, hence the awkwardness. He'd been tracking the progress on the murders in the news and seemed certain Ellen had inside information. To a degree, she did, but she had no desire to tell him.

"I read in today's paper the police are considering the two murders could be related. Have you heard anything about that?"

"The women knew each other, so it's possible."

"Yeah, the news report said that, but do you think there's any proof the same person killed both women? I'd hate to think there's a serial killer on the loose. I notice they're not saying much about Gabriel Duncan anymore. I guess he's in the clear?" John pressed. "The reports say he was questioned and released but don't provide any details."

"As far as I know, the police are still investigating. I guess they won't clear anyone without confirming alibis and whatever other evidence they have. They don't tell Gabe anything, which means he has nothing to tell me. I only know as much as anyone who reads the paper or listens to the news."

His face fell in disappointment. "Well, I guess it's normal to want to play armchair sleuth when it's so close to home."

Startled, she said, "Close to home? Did you know both women?"

He shook his head. "Physically close to home. And you and Gabriel knew both these women. That makes one degree of separation from me, eh?"

A gruesome way to view it, but she supposed he was right. "I don't think you have anything to worry about." She laughed to show how absurd the notion was and changed the subject again. "Will you take any vacation time this winter? Are you one of those

Canadians who likes to escape the cold every year?"

"Always," he replied. "Can't get enough sun and sand. I take every opportunity to get away. How about you?"

"Sure. I don't get many opportunities, but it's always nice to get away."

They continued to chat until Ellen called it a night and left to call a rideshare to take her home at nine o'clock. She still hadn't heard from Gabriel.

***

In the end, Gabriel told Zach the truth in exchange for a look at Francesca's personal files she kept at home. He convinced Zach the only way they'd figure out what she'd been doing and where she'd hid her funds was to view all the accounts she owned, including whatever she shared with her husband.

"She wanted kids, you know," Zach said, staring morosely into his now empty coffee cup. Next to it sat a crumb-covered plate. They'd all ordered sandwiches when they realized they'd talk through dinner.

Since neither Gabriel nor Carl replied, he pressed on. "Once she started working at BRI, she wouldn't take time off, and she stopped talking about having kids. Now I know why. If she took a leave, someone would take over her work while she was gone. Maternity leave would've finished her for sure, but she didn't even want to take a week off so we could go on a decent vacation."

"Sorry, Zach," Carl said. "I didn't know."

"What could you have done? She was stealing. Your choice would've been to report her or let her keep doing it." He shook his head, his expression a mixture of disgust and remorse. "She almost bankrupted the company."

"Zach," Gabriel cut in. "Think back. How were things at her previous job? Any idea if she did this before?"

He pondered a moment and then shook his head. "If she did, I have no idea. Probably not. She took vacations at her other job. They laid her off though. Work shortage. She was doing books in the accounting department for an auto parts company. Strikes at the automakers and a downturn in the economy caused layoffs, and she was low man on the totem pole. They scaled back in all departments and let her go." He picked up his empty cup as though about to take a sip, saw it had nothing in it, and set it down.

Carl stood and offered to get him another coffee. Zach nodded absently, and Carl walked away.

"I'm sorry for everything you've gone through," Gabriel said. "Who might she have worked with?"

"She was friends with Katrina Weever, but I guess you know that."

"Were they close friends?"

"I thought they were just work friends, not best friends. They went for drinks after work sometimes. Once a week, maybe. At least, that's what she told me they did. After all this, who the hell knows what she was up to?" For the first time, rage clouded his features. "She lied to me. She tricked me. I thought she was excelling at work." He pressed his palms on his thighs and rubbed them along the denim. "For all I know, she was cheating on me too."

"Do you think it was all to buy luxuries? Or did she have an addiction?"

"As far as I know, it was to keep us in the lifestyle

she craved. She wanted the good life. I guess that was her addiction: clothes, a nice house, a boat, a nice car." Zach met Gabriel's gaze, sorrow and regret in his eyes. "If I'd known what she did to get all that, I'd have told her not to. All I wanted was her. Kids. A little place to call our own. I don't care about all that other stuff. It was nice, sure, but not if it costs us everything. I've lost everything, Gabe."

Gabriel remained silent. He had nothing to say to that.

***

Ellen reread Gabriel's text message and sighed with relief: I'm heading home. Will fill you in at work.

She'd spent the last half hour either pacing her living room floor or leaning over the kitchen sink hoovering a bag of two-bite brownies in one bite per brownie. As soon as she received the message, she acknowledged it and put the food back in the cupboard. At least she could go to bed now.

She washed up and put her pyjamas on, but by the time she was ready for bed, she was no longer sleepy. With a sigh, she picked up her tablet so she wouldn't have to turn on any lights, climbed into bed, and accessed the e-book she was currently reading.

Her parents were already asleep. All sound from the upper level had ceased an hour ago. Their habit was to go to bed at 10:00 and get up by 6:00. Ellen's habit was to go to bed at whatever time she felt tired enough and, if she was lucky, sleep through until morning. Often, she woke again at 2:00 or 3:00 and had to read or check social media to kill time until she could fall asleep again. When the alarm woke her at 6:30, she'd drag herself from bed to start her day. Tonight felt like one of those restless nights, her mind too busy to allow her to wind down.

About twenty minutes had passed when she thought she heard a sound at her kitchen window. Was that glass breaking? Slowly, her heart thudding, she set down her tablet and picked up her phone. She called 911 while she made her way to the bedroom door and closed and locked it.

When the operator responded, she hysterically whispered her emergency into the phone, her gaze riveted on the doorknob. To her horror, it turned slowly, first one way then the other. The person on the other side rattled it gently, then more insistently. A scratching sound told her the person was now trying to pick the lock. Her terror rising, she backed away from the door.

CHAPTER 25

"Please, help me," Ellen whispered into the phone pressed to her ear. "He's trying to pick the lock on the bedroom door."

"Can you get out of the house from that room?" the operator asked, her voice calm and steadying.

Ellen ran to her bedroom window. "I'll try. Hurry. Please. If my parents come downstairs, he might hurt them."

"The police are already on their way, ma'am."

Ellen threw open the blinds. She pushed the window glass to the side, and, climbing onto the end table next to her bed, shoved the screen onto the grass. She hauled herself up and out just as the intruder burst through the door and into her room.

Without looking back, Ellen ran for the neighbour's house, clutching her phone to her ear.

Oh, God, just get him out before my parents find him or he hurts my cat.

She didn't care if the police caught him; she just wanted her parents to be safe. In the distance, she heard sirens.

***

Ellen arrived to work on time the next morning and went straight to Gabriel's office. He was already at his desk, sitting in front of his computer, a cup of coffee at his elbow.

"Hey, good morning." He rose to greet her but stopped in his tracks when he saw her expression. "What's wrong?"

She gulped, forcing down tears and hysteria. The moment she laid eyes on him, she wanted to break down and draw comfort in his arms.

"Someone broke into my home last night." Somehow, her voice came out steady, with only a hint of worry and nothing of the fear that plagued her.

"Oh, God. I'm glad you're okay. Tell me about it." He reached her and took her in his arms.

Tension immediately evaporated from her body, and she breathed normally again.

"Whoever it was got in through my kitchen window. I was awake and heard it, or the person would have made it into my room without me knowing. I don't know why he—or she—came, but all I can think about is Katrina."

"Christ. Tell me everything." He guided her to the sofa against the wall, and when she was sitting, he buzzed Mrs. Carbajal and asked her to bring them a pot of coffee.

As Ellen talked, his arm draped comfortingly across her shoulders, and she eased into him. She kept her gaze across the room, focusing on a painting he had on the opposite wall. It had already been in the office

158

when he took it over. Not an especially captivating print—it was a simple still life of a vase of sunflowers—she nevertheless used it to keep her from meeting his gaze. Whatever he felt, she didn't want to see it in his face.

The coffee and a plate of assorted pastries sat untouched on the coffee table in front of them while she told him what had happened from the moment she heard a sound in her kitchen to the moment she reached her neighbour's house and banged frantically on the door.

"He disappeared by the time the police got there. My parents never even knew anything was wrong until the police arrived." She finally turned to face him, her mouth quirking up into a half-smile. "They kicked the door down. At least by then I'd phoned my parents to tell them to stay upstairs, and I met the police when they arrived. They kicked in the front door to my parents' place and went into my apartment." She laughed. "I don't know why I'm laughing. I can't stop." She buried her face in her hands and shook with laughter. "Oh, my poor parents. They were so scared."

Gabriel pulled her into his lap. "Okay, it's okay. You're releasing stress. It'll be all right."

She instantly grew serious. "How can it ever be okay? Someone broke into my house. He probably wanted to kill me."

He wrapped his arms around her and drew her close. "Don't think it doesn't terrify me. What did the police say?"

"They dusted for prints. I called Detective Morris and made sure the officers on the scene knew it probably relates to his murder investigation. They'll give him whatever they find, I guess."

"Did you see who it was?"

"No. I just wanted out of there. If he could kill Fran and Kat, he could kill me too."

"If it was the same person."

"You can't possibly think it's a coincidence!"

"No, I don't think so." He eased her back onto the couch and handed her a cup of coffee. "Drink this. Eat something. Have you eaten today?"

She shook her head. "I wanted to get here so I could tell you what happened."

He frowned. "You should've called me last night."

"I'm sorry. It was late by the time the police left, and Mister Cuddles and I went upstairs to sleep at my parents because only cardboard covered my kitchen window. They're getting it repaired today."

"You need a security system. Especially now we know you're a target."

"They're getting that installed as well. Not sure it'll be today, but they're looking into it."

He took her hand. "Then, until it's safe for you to stay at home, you have to stay with me."

She thought about Katrina, and he must've read her mind, because he said, "If you're in my bed, I can keep a closer eye on you." He smiled, but he wasn't joking.

Ellen agreed because if she was away from home, her parents would be safer. She'd make certain they kept the door between the basement apartment and the main part of the house shut and locked at all times. Mister Cuddles could stay upstairs with them. If the intruder had been after something he thought she had rather than her, he might return, and by then, they'd have better security. But if he was after her, why? She hadn't figured out who'd killed the two women, and she hadn't discovered how Francesca had funnelled the money she'd skimmed.

She remembered to ask Gabriel how his meeting with Carl and Zach had gone. He summarized it for her and said, "I'll want you to go through her personal files. Zach has allowed us to come to his place and look at whatever she has there."

Ellen shook her head. "I don't know about that. What if he killed her? He might want to ..." She didn't want to finish the thought. This whole thing made her stomach hurt. She sighed. "I don't want to deal with this anymore."

Gabriel's arms tightened around her, and she rested her head on his shoulder. "I'm sorry I dragged you into this. If you're afraid, I understand if you want to back away from it. You don't have to go to Zach's with me. I can try to interpret whatever files he has by myself."

"No," she said. "I've gotten this far, so I'll keep going. I'm just tired and want peace."

"I get it. Listen," he said, "let's do something fun tonight. Go to a movie. We'll visit Zach's after work tomorrow. It can wait. We'll make sure your window is fixed, and the security is installed, and tonight, we'll go to the movies and forget about everything."

"That sounds wonderful," she replied. Part of her thought they were shirking their duties even though the murder investigation wasn't their responsibility. "Why do I feel so guilty for taking time off outside of work hours?"

Gabriel kissed her cheek. "You feel bad for Zach. I do too. And money might be transferring from BRI accounts into private accounts Fran owns that Zach doesn't even know exist. We'll figure it out, but not tonight." He eased away from her, and they stood. "If you're all right now, we should get to work. Something you find today could help us tomorrow night. Make a list of any money transfers that seem hinky to you. We'll see if they line up with anything we find at Zach's."

Feeling better than she had since the night before, she hugged Gabriel. They parted, and Ellen went to her office, ready to tackle whatever she might find.

CHAPTER 26

Six o'clock the next night found Gabriel and Ellen inside the apartment Zach had shared with Francesca for the last three years. He ushered them into a large living room with lavish furniture and sumptuous decor. Everything coordinated in light wood, cream walls, and soft, green accents. Ellen guessed Francesca had hired a professional to decorate it. When Zach invited them to sit down, Ellen eased herself onto a lushly padded sofa next to Gabriel.

Zach offered them coffee or tea, but neither Gabriel nor Ellen accepted. Ellen feared spilling something on the expensive furniture or carpeting, but she suspected Gabriel simply didn't feel like having anything right now. He never worried about offending people and never appeared self-conscious no matter the situation he found himself in.

"How are you keeping, Zach?" Ellen asked.

He looked healthy enough despite an aura of sorrow hanging about him. Bad enough he'd lost his wife without finding out she stole most of the money she'd made. The apartment itself was in an expensive location in the heart of downtown Toronto, and it had three bedrooms and a den.

It would've cost them over a million and then add maintenance fees ... Ellen quickly estimated a variety of expenses that went into this home. She couldn't help herself. Francesca was young, and the job she had didn't pay what she'd appeared to spend.

However she'd done it, Francesca had embezzled to get this place. Unless—

"Did Fran inherit money recently?" Ellen asked.

Zach shook his head. "I know what you're thinking when you look around here. We bought this place with money I thought we'd earned."

"I had Fran's job," Ellen whispered. "It doesn't pay enough to support this lifestyle." She hesitated again. "I appreciate you helping us figure this out, and I'd love to prove Fran did nothing wrong. Would you mind if I looked at both of your tax returns for the last three years you filed?"

"Sure. I've got her computer booted up and logged in under her user ID."

"She gave you that information?"

"Yes, but she never expected me to want to go into the financial files. She took care of all that. She'd never expect me to even understand most of it if I did open them up." He turned a pleading gaze on her. "Please, help me figure this out and then fix it. I didn't want all this if it meant we stole from anyone."

Ellen stood. "Okay, let's see what there is to see."

***

By the time eight o'clock rolled around, Ellen had not

only gone through all of Katrina's time-tracking reports but had also rooted through Francesca's desk, coat closet, and file cabinets. If there was anything to find, Ellen was determined to uncover it, and in one of the file cabinet drawers, she discovered a folder labelled "KatTech." The "Kat" on the label immediately brought Katrina to mind, so Ellen pulled the file and set it aside. She finished riffling through the rest of the folders in that drawer but found nothing as intriguing as the KatTech folder.

She closed the drawer, sat down at the desk, and opened it up. Inside, she found what appeared to be an itinerary, in Francesca's name, for a trip to Las Vegas, scheduled for four days in early December. Documents showed hotels, flights, and scheduled meetings with a variety of people she listed under the heading "Potential Investments."

Francesca planned to take a four-day business trip to Las Vegas? Ellen had never heard of KatTech, so if they were clients of BRI's, they were new to the company, and she didn't see mention of them in the folder. But if this was business, then why would Francesca book this over a weekend? It looked as if this was personal business, and she was using vacation days to go.

But I thought she didn't take time off? Ellen logged into BRI remotely and opened the company database. She retrieved all records that showed any time off Francesca had taken from the time she started working at BRI. They weren't many, and at the most, she took two days off, all coinciding with weekends. Ellen checked the days shown on the itinerary and verified that two of them were on a Saturday and Sunday.

Of course. If she only took a day or two during the week, she could either file whatever she needed to before she went away, file remotely while away, or catch up when she returned. She'd never need to get anyone to replace her during her absence.

Clever. This way, no one else looks at BRI's financials but her. It was a lot of power for one controller to hold. When Ellen had worked at BRI, she'd had others on staff who could take over her more critical duties when she went away for a whole week or more. If Francesca never took time off, she'd never need to ask anyone to back her up. Ever.

No wonder she'd gotten away with it for so long. Now to find out where KatTech fell in the database.

Ellen went back to work but wasn't at it for long when she heard a tapping on the office door, and Gabriel stuck his head in.

"Hey, anything I can do to help?"

"Where's Zach?" She kept her tone low and peered over Gabriel's shoulder. No sign of Zach.

"Living room. I'm hoping we can leave soon. He's tolerating the intrusion, but I can tell he's anxious to hear a report on what you've found."

"Okay, I'll wrap it up, but first, come see this. I've found something interesting." She told him about the folder she'd found and the itinerary for Las Vegas. "So far, I haven't found anything on KatTech in BRI's database."

She sifted through the documents in the folder again, looking more closely at the pages relating to the hotel Francesca planned to stay at. "It's a trade show."

"What is?"

"She's attending a trade show at the Desert Island Hotel in Vegas."

"What kind of trade show?"

Ellen scanned the documents. "Software. The list

she'd compiled of people she wanted to meet with said 'potential investments.' I think she was scouting for a business to back."

Gabriel's face registered shock as he realized what this implied. "To launder her money? How the hell much did she steal?" Anger clouded his face. "She destroyed this business for personal gain. They came close to bankruptcy."

"I know." Ellen couldn't think of anything helpful to say but felt the need to validate his outrage.

Suddenly, a look of delight crossed Gabriel's face. "Interesting. Las Vegas, eh? Are you thinking what I'm thinking?" he teased.

"God, I hope not," Ellen replied. "Unless you're thinking we need to turn this all over to Detective Morris."

"I'm thinking we need to find out what those meetings are for and who's going to show up."

"We're not going to Las Vegas," she said, but her voice betrayed her doubt.

"We're going to Las Vegas, baby."

"We can't. Whoever she was meeting could be her killer."

"That's why we have to go. Besides, that doesn't track. She already knew her killer, and he's in Toronto—likely lives here, partnered with her in the thefts. In Vegas, she wanted to find a company to invest in to clean her dirty money."

Ellen pushed her chair away from her desk and stood up. "Or they're in on it with her and taking a cut of the money she'd bring in. Detective Morris can go."

"What's he going to find out? If you're right, they'll take one look at the detective, clam up, and leave town. We'll never see them again. Besides, isn't this a jurisdictional thing? He wouldn't be able to do squat there. It's not even his country, never mind his province—state—whatever."

"We can't do this. It's too risky. And he can ask the police there to cooperate with his investigation."

"I'm going, Ellen. Come with me. We could use a trip. We'll make it a vacation. Two of those days she's booked off are on a weekend. Besides, maybe Morris will catch the killer by then, and we'll only be finding out she had some side business. We'll probably be safer there than we are here with a killer on the loose."

"You think she might have wanted to start a side business in Las Vegas?"

"Not start one but find one there. BRI has a table there. She might've talked her way into representing the company at the show, except I terminated her employment so that was no longer an option. That means she planned to go for her own reasons."

"Maybe."

"Someone is still ripping off this company. She's set up automatic withdrawals, and they're still collecting."

"I haven't seen anything like that, but I'll take a closer look tomorrow."

"Take a closer look right now. Let's open up the database and find out if KatTech is in there. I can't help associating the 'Kat' with Katrina," he said.

Ellen nodded. "That was my first thought too." She sat in her chair again and pulled up close to the desk. She accessed the database again and continued the search for any instance of KatTech.

CHAPTER 27

They didn't find KatTech in the database, so they both concluded it could be a name Francesca planned to use for her money laundering company.

"For someone so young, she sure took a lot of steps to destroy her life. Did she really think she'd get away with this long-term?" Ellen asked as she shut down the computer.

"White-collar criminals don't think about getting caught. Yeah, she likely figured she'd get away with it for as long as she wanted to. There's a good chance she'd have done this somewhere else after she left here." He contemplated a moment, then asked, "If I wouldn't have asked you to examine the previous years' files, would you have?"

"You mean as a matter of course?" Would she have dug into this if she hadn't been given the order to do so? "Yes, because when I worked here, BRI wasn't hemorrhaging money. I'd have needed to know what caused a downturn after so many profitable years."

"So, she'd have been found out either way."

"Yes, but if you hadn't hired me to do this, another person might not have done so."

"Except that whether I hired you, specifically, or not, I wanted the accounts examined."

Ellen nodded. "Because you were a client here and knew the company's history. Do you think whoever killed Fran realized all that and wanted to silence her before she was found out and arrested? If she were arrested, she'd have implicated her partners to cut a deal, don't you think?"

"Yeah, that's exactly what I think. It's what we've suspected all along. These plans don't indicate a woman about to take her own life."

"No. I guess we'd better book a trip to Las Vegas." The prospect of four days in a warmer place suddenly sounded like the perfect escape from not only the cold and snow in Ontario but also the murder investigation. Unless the killer had been part of the plan to find an investment. But if that were the case, they might flush him out and identify him for the police.

"We'd have to be careful."

Gabriel smiled. "I'm always careful."

***

With approval from Zach, Ellen copied some of Francesca's more interesting files and would take them to the office the next day to see if any of the account numbers she'd found matched accounts listed as suppliers or contractors in the ledger at BRI. When Zach asked her if she'd found anything revealing, she didn't hesitate to tell him the bad news.

"Your income for the last three years you filed was much less than Fran's. Her salary appears to be boosted by a side business she claims as consulting income, but even that doesn't explain all the money you've spent when I look at the purchases you've made. She drew funds from somewhere else but didn't claim it if it was acquired during those tax periods. It'll take me a while to investigate this and figure out how it ties to BRI and their inflated expenses. It's a breadcrumb trail I've got to follow, but she's done a good job of covering her tracks." She took his hands in hers. "I'm sorry, Zach, both for your loss and for the problems Fran left you."

"Thank you."

He invited them to stay for a drink, but all Ellen wanted to do was escape from the whole awkward situation. Gabriel, however, accepted the offer, and Zach poured Ellen a glass of red wine and got a beer for himself and Gabriel. When they were all seated, Ellen perched on the edge of the sofa with a solid grip on her wineglass.

Zach said, "Thanks for staying. It's tough to be here alone. All I do is think about her, and then instead of grieving, I get angry at what she caused."

"That's understandable," Gabriel replied.

"She loved you," Ellen added, relieved now they'd stayed because she could finally say something good about Francesca. "She talked about you all the time when we worked together. I'm so sorry she wasn't the person you thought she was, but for what it's worth, she loved you a lot. I wish I could've stopped her from doing this, but I had no idea she intended to steal." When something occurred to her, she added, "We didn't find any indication she's done this before. What changed for her, or for you guys, three years ago that might've triggered her decision?"

Zach thought about it. "Well, she lost her job, but it didn't faze her. At least, she showed no indication it bothered her at all. She'd been working at that company for over six years and wanted to sue for more severance, but it didn't work out. The lawyer told her she hadn't been working there long enough to make a lawsuit worthwhile, and they'd given her a generous severance. Maybe that angered her enough she decided she'd never give her loyalty to another company again. I know she was angry they cut her loose even though, from a business perspective, it was the right decision for the company."

"That's all it was? Resentment at having been let go?"

Zach shook his head. "I can't say. Whatever she thought about the situation, she didn't share it with me—not the truth, obviously. She complained, she tried to take action against them—and Fran always felt the need to act, to do something. She hated not being in control of her life."

"Everyone hates that feeling of being out of control in life, but it's something you have to accept," Ellen said. "Was she the vengeful type?"

"No, and this wouldn't be revenge because BRI didn't lay her off. If everything you say is true, she stole from them before Gabriel bought the place and let her go."

"Was she angry and resentful about that?" Gabriel asked, looking uncomfortable. "I gave her a substantial package."

"You did, and I appreciated that. I thought she did too. She seemed satisfied with it."

"She apply for any new jobs?"

"No. She said she had an idea for going into

business for herself."

Ellen thought about the trip to Las Vegas. Francesca had booked that before she was let go from BRI, so perhaps she'd wanted to quit her job anyway. Rumours of the buyout must've circulated, and she would've acted on those rumours if she was as proactive as Zach had claimed. Then, wouldn't her co-conspirator—or co-conspirators—have also expected the layoff? They'd have prepared for it, probably adjusting any sketchy transactions Francesca hadn't closed off.

The problem was, Ellen didn't know when Fran saw the end of her BRI career looming and started covering her tracks. This would make the search for evidence more difficult but not impossible. The trip to Las Vegas was critical.

Anxious now to leave, Ellen steered the conversation to saying goodnight to Zach, and the couple headed to Gabriel's apartment. At home, they firmed up their plans for Las Vegas over a cup of tea before bed. Gabriel said he'd put in a formal request to Carol to send Ellen to the trade show with him, and he'd pay all the expenses.

"She'll say yes to that, considering you'd also have to pay for any billable hours I spend there."

"I don't care. I'll make the arrangements, and you track your hours and submit them to your company. But I want to book the flight, the hotel, and get our passes for the trade show." He slanted her a look. "I think it would be best if we shared a room while there."

"Do you now?" She straightened her back and swivelled to face him.

He held a hand up in protest. "It's not what you think."

"Then what is it?"

"It's possible the killer will be there. I'm not letting you out of my sight."

She took a small sip of her tea. "I can take care of myself."

"It won't be a problem," he replied. "We'll stick together. Always. Agreed?"

"Agreed."

When his phone rang, he glanced at the call display. "My dad," he told her.

She almost told him to say "hi," but she didn't want to betray her resentment over living with Gabriel, no matter how temporarily, and still not having met any of his family. Instead, Ellen rose and went into the bedroom to get ready for bed so the man she loved could have his privacy.

CHAPTER 28

The moment the bedroom door closed behind Ellen, Gabriel answered the call.

"How can I help you, Dad?"

"Funny you should ask," his father replied, humour colouring his voice. "I've got an exciting proposition for you."

Gabriel's lips twisted into a frown. The last time his father had sounded this jovial, he'd sent Gabriel to London. He waited, letting his father take his time getting to whatever it was he wanted now.

"You liked London, didn't you? Had a great time? Well, guess what?"

Gabe opened his mouth to respond, but his father didn't give him the chance.

"You're going back. I've taken over a small company there, and I want you to return and get it running at a profit."

Gabriel opened his mouth to protest, but once again, his father bulldozed over him.

"I know what you're going to say. You just bought

this company and you're trying to get it going. It's your thing, and you're great at it, which is why I want you back in London. Get someone to run BRI, and you can fly back every month or so to make sure he's doing all right." Finally, Charles Duncan paused, and his son jumped into the conversation.

"Dad, I'm not leaving here. I'm getting my life back. I got my girlfriend back. I won't leave again."

"Get your priorities straight. I need you in London."

"What about Rick?" Gabriel asked, referring to his younger brother.

"Great idea. Rick would be perfect to run BRI for you. Get things in order there—you'd need, what? Three more months? Then, turn it over to Rick, and go to London. My deal won't close until six months from now anyway. You don't need to leave immediately."

How considerate. Gabriel's jaw clenched. To end the conversation, he said, "I'll think about it, Dad."

After disconnecting the call, Gabriel did just that but without making a decision. When he finally joined Ellen in the bedroom, she was already asleep, much to his relief. He wasn't prepared to mention the phone call to her.

We'll have that conversation when I've figured out my priorities. As soon as the thought left his head, he froze. What was worse: telling Ellen his father wanted him back in London or admitting to himself he'd just sounded exactly like his father?

***

Snow fell on the mid-December morning Gabriel and Ellen went to the airport to catch their flight to Las

Vegas but not enough to delay the flight. The last few days had been hectic and unfruitful. She still searched Francesca's accounts without finding definitive proof of how and to where she'd funnelled the money though Ellen sensed she was getting closer. All she had to do was locate the numbered accounts that matched account numbers Francesca's funds transferred from, but it wasn't as simple as it sounded. Francesca had covered the evidence well, and in the last few weeks of her employment, the rate of transfers had dropped significantly.

Yet Zach's heavy bills continued to get paid, and even he didn't know from where the money came. He'd listed his apartment for sale, eager to get rid of it for many reasons but mainly because it was a constant reminder of Francesca's illegal activities.

As Gabriel and Ellen waited for the plane to get clearance for takeoff, she studied her nearby fellow passengers. From the moment she and Gabriel had arrived at the gate, she'd tried to determine if anyone boarding their plane looked familiar or noticed the BRI couple.

They had booked the same flight Francesca would've taken. If her partner had killed her, it was possible he—or she—sat on this very flight. The prospect that the killer could be on the plane with them filled Ellen's stomach with butterflies, but so far, no one raised her suspicions.

"He could've taken a different flight," Ellen whispered to Gabriel. The two sat in first-class seats, and as each person boarded, she watched them closely as they passed by. No one looked either familiar or suspicious.

"Who?" he whispered back.

"Fran's partner."

"If he's smart, he won't go at all," he replied.

"And lose the deal they were going to make?"

"Deals come and go. There'll be other trade shows. If he shows up in Vegas, we'll recognize him, or Morris will check flight schedules and cross-reference them with his suspect list—which we're probably still on."

"What?" His words sent a wave of shock through her.

"He won't trust we're in the clear. Fran was killed in the middle of the day. I have an alibi for some of that time, but for much of that day, I was working from home—alone."

This was the first Ellen had heard that, and a surge of fear followed the shock.

Gabriel isn't a killer, she reminded herself and shook off the thought he might have lured her to Las Vegas to kill her. Otherwise, she'd run screaming from the plane. He didn't have an alibi for Katrina's death either. As a matter of fact, he'd been in the apartment with her. The plane suddenly felt icy, and Ellen shivered.

"Did you tell Detective Morris we were leaving the country?" Ellen asked. She should've done that herself.

"Yes. It's fine."

"Did you tell him why?"

"I told him we were attending a trade show."

"But not that we were following up in case Fran was meeting her partner here or investing to launder her money?"

"Of course not. Not without proof of that. The last thing we need is a cop following us out here." He squinted at her, examining her expression. "What's wrong?"

"Nothing." She averted her eyes and quieted as the

plane taxied along the runway, picked up speed, and then lifted off the ground. She always hated takeoffs and landings. Statistically, these were the most dangerous times during the flight, but she never relaxed enough during any part of a flight to enjoy it. All she wanted now was the bar cart to come around.

Gabriel didn't let it drop. "Something's bothering you. I can tell."

"I'm nervous. You should know that about me. I hate flying."

"Okay," he said, "I'll buy that." But his dubious expression told her he didn't.

By now, though, she'd come to her senses—at least, she assured herself she'd come to her senses. How could Gabriel be the killer? He'd never met Francesca, and if he'd been her partner in crime, he'd never have fired her. She'd still be doing the books at BRI.

Unless he fired her and killed her because her theft was becoming noticeable by putting the company under financial strain. Again, she dismissed the notion. None of that made sense. Gabriel wasn't stupid. He wouldn't doggedly have Ellen investigate the accounts if he were behind the whole thing.

She took his hand, guilt making her want to atone for her disloyal thoughts. He threw her a startled glance and then relaxed into a smile that warmed her heart.

He has nothing to do with this. How could I even consider it? Having him back in her life had been wonderful despite the problems they'd faced. It wasn't his fault Francesca had stolen from the company and that someone had murdered her.

And Katrina. Someone had also murdered her, and Ellen had yet to understand how the young woman related to this mess. Ellen had dug into BRI's payments to the software developer, and none of them had been suspiciously large. She'd also looked up Katrina's home address and discovered she rented a small one-bedroom apartment just north of Toronto. If she was spending ill-gotten gains, it didn't show anywhere Ellen could see.

She relaxed, as much as she could relax on a flight, when the bar cart appeared and the flight attendant gave her the red wine she ordered. Gabriel accepted a whisky. The flight would last roughly five hours, arriving in Las Vegas shortly after noon Nevada time.

Gabriel pulled out his laptop, and she watched him boot it up and settle into whatever office work he'd brought with him. *Not a bad idea.* Ellen removed her laptop from its bag and booted it up. If she was lucky, maybe she'd find useful information by the time they arrived in Vegas. She daydreamed about calling Detective Morris when they landed and telling him who she suspected was the killer. But when they landed, she was no closer to revealing the killer than she had been when they'd left.

***

Their suite at the Desert Island had a separate living area with a wet bar, a powder room off the living area, an en suite bathroom off the master bedroom, and floor-to-ceiling windows that afforded a view of the airport and Strip over fifty stories below.

Ellen had never stayed in a place so expensive and opulent. She spotted at least three televisions distributed throughout the over one-thousand-square-foot area. There was enough seating to entertain a crowd of guests. The colour scheme seemed outdated—lots of mauves and purples—but it was tasteful. The padded sofas, chairs, and love seats looked comfortable enough to settle in with a good book. Vases of flowers adorned the tabletops, and a bottle of champagne chilled in a bucket next to a basket of fruit and chocolates on the kitchen table.

"Do you come here often?" she asked, thinking management was rewarding him for his patronage.

"Often enough."

The space and number of seats also threw her off the more she investigated the unit and found it worthy of entertaining a crowd.

"Are we having a party I don't know about?" she asked when they'd finished settling in.

Gabriel laughed. "No. I like my space."

"Sure you do." She wouldn't mind a party under normal circumstances but not with a killer on the loose. No matter how hard she tried, she couldn't shake the feeling that whoever had killed Francesca and Katrina knew they were here and would hunt them down.

"What would you like to do first?" he asked. "The trade show doesn't start until tomorrow, so we've got all afternoon free." He opened his suitcase and removed a penknife from an inside pocket.

"What's that for?"

"Whatever." He slipped it into his pants pocket. "I always carry it, but I had to put it into my suitcase for the flight. Kinda feel naked without it."

"Okay."

He gave her a sheepish look. "My dad gave it to me when I was a kid. Sentimental value, I suppose. Want to go gamble?"

She thought about her insanely high credit card bills. "I should skip that. Much as I'd like to win enough to pay off all my debts, I'd probably lose it all and then have no spending money left. Why don't we walk along the Strip? I've never been to Vegas before. It'd be nice to scope things out." She'd glimpsed the Strip from the plane and couldn't wait to walk through it all. The hotel lobby alone had left her bug-eyed and excited to see everything.

December temperatures in Las Vegas were chillier than they would be the rest of the year, so Ellen had packed warm clothes, but it wouldn't get anywhere near as cold here as it was back in Toronto. Cold here meant fifty to sixty degrees Fahrenheit. Cold in Toronto meant minus twenty Celsius though they likely wouldn't hit that low until January or February. All this could be over by then, and she and Gabriel could take a real vacation somewhere tropical. She thought about Francesca, who'd given up taking vacations and even starting a family because money and possessions were more important to her than either of those things.

Gabriel agreed to take a walk, and they changed into jeans and T-shirts. Ellen topped hers with a sweater, and Gabriel put on a light windbreaker. The current temperature was sixty-two, which, for the two Canadians, was positively balmy at this time of year. They rode the elevator to the lobby, and as they walked arm in arm past the registration desks toward the exits, Ellen heard her name called. A sinking feeling in her gut, she tightened her grip on Gabriel's arm and turned to face Rhonda.

CHAPTER 29

"Hey! What are you two doing here?" Rhonda shouted, turning heads her way as everyone who heard her holler wondered if someone they knew hailed them. She had her arm hooked through Max's, and next to them stood John and a woman Ellen didn't recognize.

"Us? What are you doing here?" Ellen hadn't told Rhonda she and Gabriel were travelling to Vegas because they wanted to keep the trip a secret. The sight of her friend shocked and worried Ellen. Surely, Rhonda had nothing to do with Francesca and her shady dealings.

Ellen and Gabriel strolled over to the two couples, and Ellen and Rhonda hugged one another.

"The software trade show. Max talked me into coming down with him. He's interested in checking out the latest software for law offices. He and John booked this a while ago. I was a last-minute addition. How come you never mentioned coming?"

"How come you didn't?" Ellen hedged.

"Didn't get a chance. Once we decided I'd come

along, I was frantically trying to book time off work, get ahead in my accounts so no one would miss me, and prepare for the trip. I only booked my ticket a week ago."

"Yeah, me too. Gabriel was attending and invited me along." Which was almost true enough. "I guess this show must be popular."

"Oh, I'm so rude," Rhonda declared. "You haven't even met Luanne. She works with John." Rhonda introduced them to John's companion, a tall, leggy redhead with a pale complexion and an aura of sophistication. She wore a business casual pantsuit, and the gems in the jewellery she sported looked genuine and expensive. She stood slightly apart from John as though to signify to the world they weren't together.

John smiled shyly at Ellen and gave her a brief hug. "Nice to see you," he whispered in her ear.

"You too," she replied as they parted. To the group, she said, "When did you all arrive?"

"Yesterday," Max said.

"And you're all staying here at the Desert Island?" Gabriel asked.

"Yes. And you're here for the trade show." Rhonda riveted her gaze on Ellen as she spoke.

Resentment bubbled up at Rhonda's persistence in questioning their presence here, but Ellen shrugged it off as best she could and said, "They offer accounting software my company wants me to vet, and BRI has a table here for their reporting software and proprietary coding services."

John's stare pinned Ellen as if it were a spotlight, and she tried to keep her gaze off him. He couldn't possibly think she'd led him on. From her periphery, she scoped out his expression but couldn't interpret what he might be thinking. It was obvious she and Gabriel were more than just business associates, but she'd already explained to John she wasn't interested in getting involved with him on an intimate level. She smoothed away the frown that kept wanting to spring to her face and betray her frustration.

"Where are you heading?" Max asked. "Care to join us in the casino?"

"Thank you, no," Ellen replied before Gabriel could say anything. She wanted to speak to him in private and to spend as little time in John's company as possible. In a way, she was sorry about that. If it weren't for Gabriel and the deep rapport they'd established four years ago, she might have taken an interest in the other man.

She immediately caught herself in the lie. No, however attractive he was and however successful he was, they had next to nothing in common. They would've shared a few interesting dates and possibly some good sex, but she was sure a relationship with him couldn't last. Better for both of them to avoid that kind of entanglement. Hopefully, he'd realize that over time.

When Rhonda next suggested they meet for dinner, Ellen couldn't say no. She and Gabriel agreed to meet them at the Irish pub and restaurant in New York-New York for six o'clock, and they parted company. As soon as they stepped through the exits onto the sunny sidewalk, Ellen took Gabriel aside so they wouldn't interfere with the rest of the pedestrian traffic and said, "I swear I didn't know Rhonda was coming."

"I could see that. You looked positively gobsmacked." His voice and expression held amusement.

"That's not funny. She didn't know Francesca, to my knowledge, but she knew *of* her. I'm Rhonda's connection to Francesca and to Katrina."

Gabriel's jaw dropped and his eyes widened. "You're not saying you think your friend killed them."

"No." So what was her point? "I'm not sure what I'm getting at."

"You heard her yourself. She's here as a last-minute add-on. Max invited her because they've gotten close over the last two months."

Ellen nodded. "It's the longest relationship Rhonda's had in a long time, to be honest. She considers herself picky, but I think she's afraid to commit. When they're together, they seem to have something I've never seen her have with anyone else. Frankly, he makes her happy, and I hope it works out." Her jaw dropped as a terrible thought occurred to her. "You don't think Max ..." She refused to finish the statement, but Gabriel completed it for her.

"Killed Fran and Kat? How could he have known them?"

"I don't know," Ellen said, "but we'd better find out. If he knew them, he might be our killer. He could be the one meeting that investor, and he invited Rhonda and John along as cover."

Gabriel considered in silence, then said, "Or John did."

Ellen's heart almost stopped, and her eyes held panic as she gripped Gabriel's arm with both hands.

"Fran consulted a labour lawyer before." She gulped. "Dear God, what if he's the one who compelled her to steal, and that's why she never did it before she started working at BRI. She met him when she sued her previous company."

"Now, you're jumping to conclusions. We can't assume anything—not even that it's someone we know. Trust me, I know this from experience." The smile he flashed calmed her and she returned it with genuine warmth and relief.

"You're right. We'll have to find proof. Call Zach and ask him to find out the name of the labour lawyer Fran used."

He patted her arm. "Okay. Let's walk, enjoy ourselves for a bit. We're meeting them for dinner. We'll get him to divulge he knew the women."

"That's the thing. He already told me he didn't. We can't just ask him. If we find out he lied, we'll know he's the one." And she'd spent time alone with him, had invited him to her home. It would've made breaking into her house easier, since he knew the layout of her apartment and that it was separate from her parents' unit.

"What if Max is in on it too?" Her chest heaved, and Gabriel cupped her face in his hands.

"Slow down, Ellen. You're hyperventilating. You'll make yourself pass out." He kissed her lips, a gentle mouth-to-mouth that resuscitated her and slowed her breathing to a more tolerable rate.

"I'm okay." She took his hand in hers and strolled along the wide walkway. "Look." She pointed. "Dragons."

On either side of the path stood what looked like gigantic dragons carved from stone and sitting on concrete pedestals that bore the name of the hotel.

"Not sure the heads look the way I picture a dragon head, but I guess that's what they're supposed to be," he remarked.

She appreciated how easily he accepted the

diversion. "Take a photo of me in front of this one."
She sidled up to the pedestal, the dragon looming out
of reach above her. In front of her, lush green foliage
grew in a landscaped plot and beside that stood a
turquoise street lamp structure, ornately carved with
four lamps curling up and out from the top.

"All right." To his credit, he didn't question the
timing or why she'd want to do this. He held up his cell
phone. "Ready?"

When she nodded and smiled, he snapped the
photo. "Got it."

With a glance over her shoulder at the hotel where
Rhonda and her group remained, Ellen plastered a
smile on her face and said, "Let's have some fun."

CHAPTER 30

Three hours later, Ellen and Gabriel arrived back at their hotel room to get ready to meet Rhonda and her group for dinner. Ellen had done some shopping, which added to her credit card load, but she couldn't resist buying a few items of clothing and jewellery for herself and a bottle of Nevada vodka and some poker chips and dice for Gabriel. The chips for Gabriel were custom clay chips, and Ellen, for once in her life, didn't blink at the price or consider the gift an obligation or chore. All she wanted was to see the look of delight on his face when she gave him the gifts, which she planned to do at Christmas.

She recalled with pride and amusement how sneaky she'd been, asking one sales clerk to distract him while she purchased the gifts from another clerk. The whole enterprise had been fun and exciting, and she suddenly understood why people who gave gifts enjoyed it. She set her bags down next to her side of the bed, and when Gabriel was in the living room occupied with calling Zach, she slipped her purchases into her suitcase.

"What did he say?" she asked, stepping from the bedroom. Unable to help the cat-that-ate-the-canary grin on her face, she kept her back to him and fixed herself a drink at the bar.

"Didn't talk to him."

Her grin vanished and she whirled around to face him. "Why?"

"I had to leave a voicemail, but I'm sure he'll get back to me. I told him it was important."

Ellen frowned but kept her concerns to herself. What could a few hours or even a day matter? They'd just have to be cautious, stick together, and avoid being alone with John. That should be easy enough to do.

Promptly at 5:50, Ellen and Gabriel left the room, Ellen hanging the "Do not disturb" sign on the outside door handle.

"What's that for?" Gabriel asked, a half-smile on his lips.

"To fool burglars."

The smile widened to unrestrained amusement. "How will it do that?"

"Trust me. It'll make them think we're in there getting it on, and they'll pass us by. We'll leave it out unless we're both in the room."

The grin became a chuckle, and he patted his belly as if soothing an ache from too much merriment. "That's awesome."

"Glad you're entertained." But she met him grin for grin. Taking his hand, she led him to the elevators.

They entered the Irish pub at the New York-New York hotel twenty minutes later. Ellen's nerves kicked in as the pair approached the table where Max and Rhonda sat. John and Luanne were nowhere in sight. As soon as she sat down, Ellen turned a questioning eye on Rhonda.

"Where are John and Luanne?" The two hadn't appeared to be a couple, but Ellen might've assessed the situation incorrectly. In that case, maybe they should suspect Luanne along with John.

What the hell? Does he have a harem of women stealing for him? He's not that charming.

"Luanne had a date, and John wanted to gamble more. I think he's got a streak going. He said he'd eat later." Rhonda laughed, and the mirth reached her eyes.

Ellen didn't find this news amusing at all. John knew she and Gabriel were occupied having dinner with Max and Rhonda. He could do anything during that time, and they wouldn't know what he was up to.

Ellen almost laughed out loud. What did she think he'd do with this hour or two of freedom? Break into their room? Put out a contract on them? Her suspicions sounded ludicrous even to her.

She settled into her seat, picked up her menu, and turned to Gabriel. "What shall we have to drink? Want to split a bottle of wine?"

He preferred to sample one of the Irish beers they offered, so Ellen ordered a glass of white wine. Red wine didn't appear to be on the menu, so she ordered something she'd never tried.

The meal passed pleasantly enough, and Ellen could almost forget a killer lurked in their midst. After they'd eaten their food and drank everything they'd ordered, Max suggested they take a stroll around the hotels.

"Rhonda's never been to Vegas before. This is all new to her."

"To me too," Ellen said. "I'd love to explore the Luxor and the other nearby hotels. They all look so fascinatingly gaudy." She laughed. The alcohol she'd drank gave her a pleasant buzz.

Gabriel's brows shot up in puzzlement, but she simply smiled at him and patted his thigh. "It'll be fun." She turned to Rhonda. "I have to hit the ladies' room before we go. Care to join me?"

"Sure." Her friend rose and said to the men, "We'll be back in a minute."

"I doubt that." Max chuckled. Gabriel followed suit though he frowned, a look that hinted at worry rather than disapproval.

As soon as they reached the women's washroom, Rhonda did a quick check of the area. Two stalls were occupied, and one woman washed her hands at the sink. Rhonda pulled Ellen to one side.

"Why didn't you text me to tell me you guys were coming to Vegas?"

"Why didn't you text me?" Ellen replied.

"I'm sorry. It went so quickly. I kept meaning to let you know, but every time I thought about it, it was inconvenient. Next thing I know, we're here and you're stepping off the elevator with Gabe."

"You could've texted me last night." Both kept their voices low, as if the other women in the bathroom might care what they said.

"Yes, I'm sorry. I didn't think of it. We've been busy." Rhonda's eyes lit up with excitement. "Max and I explored the Strip, had dinner at a really nice restaurant at the Desert Island, and went to a show."

"Did John and Luanne go with you?"

Rhonda's brows arched and her mouth quirked up. "You jealous?"

"I'm curious. What's the story with him and Luanne?"

"She's an assistant at his law firm, like I told you."

"Yeah, but what was she doing with John if she's seeing someone else?"

Rhonda laughed. "Just hanging out."

Ellen didn't buy it. "Has she just hung out with him a lot here?"

"I thought you weren't jealous?"

"I'm not."

They fell silent as the woman who'd been washing her hands finished drying them under the hand dryer and left the bathroom. One woman exited her stall and turned on the tap at the sink. Ellen turned her attention back to Rhonda.

"This might sound crazy, but what do you know about John? What do you even know about Max?"

Rhonda stared at her, puzzled. "What's that supposed to mean?"

"Nothing. I'm concerned you might be involved with someone whose friend ..." She trailed off. How could she bring herself to say it? Should she say it? Rhonda wouldn't be in on it, but revealing to her friend that John might be the killer could put her in jeopardy. Yet keeping her ignorant could also put her in jeopardy.

"Whose friend what, Ellen? Finish what you started to say." Rhonda's voice had grown louder, and Ellen put a placating hand on her friend's arm.

"Shh," she warned, inclining her head in the direction of the stalls.

The bathroom door opened, and another woman entered and headed into a stall. The handwashing woman finished at the dryer and left. The closed stall remained closed, the woman in it continuing to sit. Her running-shoe-clad feet were visible under the stall's door.

That must be some massive dump she's having. Hope she's okay. The air remained blessedly odour free, however, much to Ellen's relief. She turned back to her friend.

"Has John ever given you any reason to distrust him?"

"No!" Rhonda snapped the response out and, grabbing Ellen by the arm, pulled her farther from earshot of the women in the main part of the bathroom. "What do you think he's done?"

"Nothing. I'm sorry." She thought back to the night they all met. John had deliberately avoided sitting next to Rhonda—he'd steered her in Max's direction and made certain Ellen sat beside him. At least, that's how it looked to her upon reflection. What if it wasn't because he'd found her more attractive than her friend? Afraid to say that out loud, she simply said, "I'm really sorry. You're here with these two men, and you don't know them too well."

"Oh, well, isn't that nice? Max has been amazing from the moment we met. He hasn't forced anything on me. John has been nice and pleasant, and if he's Max's friend, then I trust him, because Max has excellent judgment. He's a prosecutor, for God's sake. He puts away the bad guys." She dropped her hands from Ellen.

"As I recall, you considered the possibility Gabe killed Katrina," Ellen reminded her friend.

"Katrina was killed when she was alone with him in his apartment. If anyone's dating a killer, it's you, but you won't consider that, will you?" Rhonda retorted, continuing to keep her voice low, but her face contorted in rage. She huffed out an exasperated breath and said, "I came in here to use the washroom. I'll see you around." She stalked into a stall and shut the door.

Since Ellen was here anyway, she entered a stall and used the toilet. When she came out, she saw the stall Rhonda had gone into was empty, and her friend wasn't at the sink or the hand dryer either. The running-shoe-clad feet were also gone. Ellen quickly washed her hands and hurried from the bathroom.

When she arrived back at their table, she found it empty.

CHAPTER 31

Ellen scanned the restaurant, searching frantically for Gabriel, Rhonda, or Max. She stood next to the table, trying to figure out what could've happened. Was Rhonda so angry she'd stormed from the restaurant, taking Max with her? And taking Gabriel as well? How could he leave her? What could Rhonda have said to make him abandon her?

No, it's a mistake. He's in the washroom. I just have to wait for him to return.

She sat down at the table, which still held their dirty dishes and empty glasses. The server spotted her sitting alone and came over.

"Your party has paid the bill, ma'am," he said. "You're welcome to sit here as long as you like, but the rest of your group left."

She felt the blood drain from her face, and the server must have noticed the panic in her eyes, because he said, "The other couple left together. Your companion stepped outside to take a call. If you were expecting to leave together, I'm sure he'll be right back."

"Okay, thanks." She picked up her almost-empty water glass and took a small sip. Remembering her cell phone, she mentally kicked herself for not thinking of it immediately. She fired off a text to Gabriel: Where are you? I'm still in the restaurant, waiting for you at our table.

How could he abandon her like this? Had Rhonda told Max and Gabriel about the argument and convinced them to leave her here? Insane. *He wouldn't.*

She checked her phone. No text. Ellen clutched her purse to her stomach, folding her arms across the shiny black cloth. Had he really walked out on her in another country?

No, no. She shook her head to emphasize the point. *He wouldn't. Of course he wouldn't.* Even if he were angry with her, he wouldn't just walk away and leave her. Yet, he'd abandoned her before, and he had a tendency to jump to conclusions.

People don't change. But she had. Didn't she just today buy him presents even though she didn't have to? She'd never have done that before. Ellen rose from her seat and walked to the pub's entrance, which looked out on the resort's shopping concourse. Relief flooded through her when she spotted him disconnecting a call, and she hurried to join him.

"Did Zach return your call?" She held her breath, hoping Zach had given a different lawyer's name. *Just not John, please, don't let it be John.*

"My dad." Concern lined his face.

She released the breath she'd held, but it provided little release from the tension that tied her in knots. She'd continue to twist and worry until Zach gave them a name, and from the look of it, Gabriel's father had called with bad news.

"What's wrong? Is your dad all right?" She couldn't keep the concern from her voice.

Gabriel took her hand and led her away from the front of the restaurant. Around them, couples strolled, all looking, to Ellen's eyes, carefree and happy. They laughed and chatted or walked in companionable silence. How she envied them. Gabriel held her hand, but she picked up on the stress he carried. The silence they walked in now was laced with tension.

"He's fine," Gabriel said at last and then gave a bitter chuckle. "He's always fine."

Ellen swallowed the lump in her throat. *Bad news coming. He's going to hit me with it.* She tensed, pulled her hand from his, and stopped walking. "Tell me."

"He wants me to move back to England."

He didn't say no, or he wouldn't look as if he had something to hide. "What did you tell him?"

"Ellen, it'll be all right. I think I've figured out what we can do."

He's going. It was three years ago all over again, and this time, the separation would kill her. *How will I get over him? Why did I let him back into my life?*

"No, it's not like before," he said, guessing her thoughts.

"How isn't it like that? I can't move to England to live with you. I won't. My family and my life are here." Something else occurred to her then. "What about BRI? You just bought the company. I thought that's what you wanted for yourself. To run your own business."

"It is. Dad wants me to do that in London." Before she could respond, he said, "This time, it'll be different. We'll get married. Marry me, Ellen."

Stunned, she could only stare at him, blinking. Did he think it was as simple as that for her? That the only issue she'd had last time was he hadn't proposed?

"I can't move out of the country, Gabe. Don't you understand? My whole life is here."

He took her arm and led her toward the elevators.

She realized they'd walked back to the Desert Island. "No. I can't."

"Ellen, my life is with you. I don't want to lose you. Not again."

"Then why do you want to move to England? You said yourself you wanted to be here. You returned because your life is here."

The elevator doors opened. People shuffled off, and Gabriel took her arm again and tried to lead her inside. She pulled free and stepped away from him.

"I need to be alone." She turned her back on him and started walking, her pace slow but steady. Footsteps behind her told her he followed. She spun around. "Let me be, Gabe. I need to think, to be alone so I can figure this out."

He shook his head, his face flushing red and etched with a scowl. "I'm not letting you wander off by yourself."

She softened her voice in her reply. "I'll be fine. I'm staying in the lobby, and I'll call Rhonda." A smile flicked across her lips. "Girl talk. Best if I talk to my friend. Okay?" Except her friend was angry with her, wasn't she?

Worry about that later. If Rhonda answered her phone, Ellen could smooth things over, ask her to meet for a drink.

Gabriel frowned, hesitated. The world seemed to hang on his decision.

If he walks away, it means he trusts me. Or it meant he could abandon her again now as easily as he'd done three years ago. She shoved that ludicrous, self-sabotaging thought aside.

"I'll give you an hour, Ellen. We'll meet in our hotel room. If you're not back by then, I'm calling the cops."

A bit dramatic. But she agreed to his terms and followed him with her gaze until he'd disappeared into the elevator.

***

Since he had no idea if Ellen would take the full hour, and because he needed to clear his own head in peace and quiet, Gabriel headed up to their hotel room. As he rode up in the elevator, he considered what he'd do if she refused to move to London. He could stay in Toronto. Couldn't he?

That would disappoint his father. Gabriel visualized telling his father he refused the transfer—not that it took a great deal of effort—they'd already argued over this. His father would respond with annoyance and frustration. What Gabriel really needed to visualize was what his life in Toronto would be like if he stayed here. He might have to leave his father's company altogether, making BRI his own baby. His income would plummet, but that prospect didn't worry him. He knew he could make BRI successful, and even if his income never matched what he made working for his father, why should it matter?

Challenge motivated him, not money—and pleasing his father had motivated him. For most of Gabriel's life, getting his father's approval had mattered the most. What he realized now, as he stepped from the elevator and strode down the corridor to his suite, was that no matter how hard he tried, his father wanted more. Not that Gabriel's performance had displeased Charles. Gabriel had always performed exceptionally, had succeeded, delivered the desired results. But he never reached that moment where he'd done enough, where he'd step out from under his father's control and be his own man. That, he decided, using his key card to unlock the door, was the crux of the issue.

As he opened the door, a shove to his back had him stumbling into the hotel room.

He cursed and spun around to confront whoever had pushed him. His brain registered the gun John pointed at him. "What the hell is this?"

John kicked the "Do not disturb" sign that had slid from the door's handle into the suite, shut the door, and sneered in response. "The end of the line."

CHAPTER 32

A bench between two giant potted plants made a convenient nook in which Ellen could sit and think. She watched people stroll past and considered calling Rhonda but couldn't bring herself to make the call. One fight at a time was more than enough to deal with, and the situation with Gabriel was her priority.

But should it be? Should her lover trump her friend? Especially a lover who'd abandoned her once before under similar circumstances? Before she could change her mind, Ellen retrieved her cell phone from her purse and called Rhonda.

"Hi."

"I'm so sorry, Rhonda." Her voice pleaded forgiveness.

"You hurt me." She paused. "Do you believe Max had anything to do with Fran's and Katrina's deaths? Really?"

"No." She could honestly say she didn't. She suspected John. But the two men were best friends. Could Max really be innocent? Still, they had no proof of anything; otherwise, they'd have taken it to the police. "I didn't mean to accuse him of anything."

"I didn't mean to imply Gabe could do something like that too. We're both on edge."

Ellen considered telling Rhonda about the recent break-in at the basement apartment but thought better of it. The two never kept secrets from one another, but Ellen preferred to talk about this in person. She'd wait. At least they were back on speaking terms.

She exhaled her relief. When she spoke again, her voice sounded normal, the way it sounded whenever the two best friends talked. "Where are you?"

"We're walking on the Strip. I wanted to do some shopping. You?"

Ellen considered telling her friend what had happened but changed her mind. Let Rhonda and Max have their time together. "Returning to our hotel room. Can we meet later—just you and me? For drinks?"

"Sure." Rhonda's tone was soft, and Ellen heard the affection in it.

"Thanks. What time works for you? After dinner?" By then, she and Gabriel should've worked things out.

"Sure. How's nine o'clock? At the Desert Island Bar?"

"I'll be there." Before her friend could disconnect, Ellen said, "Rhonda?"

"Yeah?"

"Thanks. I'm really sorry."

"It's okay, Ellen. We're friends. We'll always be friends. There's nothing you can do to change that."

"Okay."

They said their goodbyes, and after disconnecting the call, Ellen slipped her phone into the front pouch of her purse. The repair to her relationship with

Rhonda gave Ellen hope she could fix things with Gabriel as well. Together, they could work something out.

He'd asked her to marry him this time. Yet, he hadn't said "I love you." The proposal implied it. She knew him well enough by now to know he loved her, and it wasn't as if she'd said the words to him even though she felt it.

With a sigh, she rose from her seat. She couldn't sit here all day. All she could think to do was return to the hotel room and discuss things with him. She rushed through the corridor, barely noticing her surroundings, moving on instinct back to the elevator.

She waited patiently for one of them to open. More happy people came and went, and when the up-elevator door opened, a jovial crowd, probably heading to the casino or to a show, stepped off. Ellen slipped inside with four other people and pressed the button to the fiftieth floor. Her heart pounded at the nagging fear this conversation would end as it had three years ago, but she tried to relax.

Things are different now. We love each other. He wants to marry me.

The others in the elevator got off before she reached her floor, so she was alone when the doors opened to let her out. She stepped into the foyer and checked the signs for the room numbers. Always a little disoriented when she stepped off an elevator, she was unsure which direction to take. Locating her room number on the sign, Ellen followed the arrows. As she neared the room, she listened for any activity anywhere. All was quiet. She slowed her pace as she approached the door to their suite.

When she flashed the access card across the

scanner, the lock beeped and flashed green. She turned the door handle, and as she stepped into the room, she realized her "Do not disturb" sign no longer hung from the handle. Ellen paused.

No, something's wrong. Go back. In that split second, someone grabbed her wrist and hauled her into the room.

"Welcome to the party," a mocking voice said.

***

All the lights were on in the suite—even those in the bedroom. The curtains were drawn over the windows, closing out the sparkle of the Las Vegas Strip at night. Ellen scanned the kitchen, the dining area, and the living room. She didn't see Gabriel, and her heart skipped a beat.

"Where's Gabe?" she asked, because that was more important at the moment than "What the hell are you doing in my room?" was.

"Bedroom."

She yanked her wrist from John's grasp and ran for the bedroom. She felt more than saw John following close behind her, but that didn't matter.

Gabriel lay on the bed, one hand cuffed to the bedpost. His mouth was stuffed with a cloth that tied behind his head, and his eyes were closed. For one heart-stopping moment, she thought he was dead.

"What have you done to him?" she shrieked and ran to his side, dropping her purse on the bed and throwing herself onto him.

"Just drugged. He'll live." After a breath, John added, "For now."

She stroked Gabriel's cheek and started to undo the

knot that held the gag in place.

"Leave it."

Ellen glared at John and for the first time realized he held a gun in his gloved hands. "What will you do? Shoot us?" As soon as the words were out, she regretted the rashness of it, but it wouldn't matter. John likely did intend to shoot them. She didn't even understand why. What had she or Gabriel done to make John turn on them? How had he known they suspected him? But she ignored his order and continued to fiddle with the gag. He didn't try to stop her again, so she considered that a win.

As the gag slipped from Gabriel's mouth, she said, "What are you doing? Why?" She thought of Rhonda, of Max. "Where are Max and Rhonda?"

"Don't worry about them."

She waited. When he didn't expand on that, she said, "What is all this?"

"Don't play stupid, Ellen. You've been interfering in everything since Gabriel Duncan took over BRI."

As if checking a sick child for a fever, she pressed a palm to Gabriel's forehead. He stirred, perhaps her cool hand helping to revive him, and she shifted to sit so she could cradle his head in her lap.

"You put the bug in his apartment." He'd heard them talking and decided they knew too much. She tried to recall what they'd said, but fear had blanked her memory. "You broke into my apartment."

His response was chillingly casual. "You should be dead already."

She met his gaze, and he returned the stare, his eyes cold steel.

"How the hell did you get in here?"

John smirked. "Easy enough once he opened the

206

door. I could see it in your eyes, Ellen. Don't ever play poker. The way you looked at me—or, rather, the way you avoided looking at me. You think I didn't know you verified I was the lawyer she consulted?"

"Zach told you?"

"He called our office to find out. My assistant called to let me know a murdered client's husband called asking for the name of the lawyer she consulted. Zach not only asked about the first case Fran called me for, but he asked about BRI. He mentioned he'd talked to Gabriel."

"So you decided the most logical thing to do was hunt us down?"

"You disappear here, no one will find you."

"Disappear?" She thought of the desert. Cliché, sure, but probably the best way to dispose of a body in this place. Tendrils of nausea wove through the pit of her stomach, the result of visions of cold, lonely stretches of desert where coyotes and other wild animals foraged.

He'd still have to get them from here to there, and the only way to do that was to walk them out at gunpoint. Killing them in the room would leave too much evidence and the problem of removing the bodies.

While there's life, there's hope.

"You're a problem for me. I can't have you taking what you know back to the cops in Toronto."

Fine. I'll take it to the cops here in Vegas. "Why kill Kat?" She didn't give him the option of denying it. "How'd you get into Gabe's apartment that night?"

"Stupid wench. She was supposed to seduce him and let me in when he fell asleep. Stupid broad made so much noise when I got there, she risked waking him

207

even after we went out on the balcony to talk. Tried to shut her up. Choked her out instead. Only thing to do after that was toss her over the side and hope they called it a suicide. You and that idiot"—he snarled in Gabriel's direction—"just couldn't leave things alone. You found the bug and went to the fucking cops. Once that cop realizes I knew both women, I'm done."

She visually examined the handcuff on the bedpost, trying to see a way to remove it, but it was clipped to a piece of the carved headboard that curled in on itself. She wouldn't be able to simply slide the cuff over the end.

"We'll take your car," he said as though they were making plans for an evening out.

"Go to hell. I'm not doing anything you want."

"I've got the gun. You know I'll use it. I've killed twice now. Twice more won't bother me."

"Is that why you sent me and Rhonda those drinks the night we met? Did you know who I was?"

"Of course. Frankly, if it had really been a meet-cute, I'd have let Rhonda sit next to me." He sneered. "Did you really think I was interested in you? You plain, chubby wreck."

Tears welled up, and she averted her eyes, staring down at Gabriel's hands and the cuffs she couldn't remove. "Take the cuffs off."

"Right away, Your Highness." He chuckled.

Since he refused to free Gabriel, Ellen shifted to sit beside him, laying his head on the pillow again. She slipped her hand into one of his, taking comfort from the physical contact. Was it her imagination, or did his hand squeeze hers for a second? She kept her face averted from John's gaze.

Keep him talking. "How did you even know Kat?"

"Shut up. I'm done talking to you. You won't live through this. Neither you nor your boyfriend."

Once again, Gabriel exerted a gentle pressure on Ellen's hand, and this time, she knew for sure she hadn't imagined it. Gabriel was awake, and he signalled her to keep the knowledge to herself.

CHAPTER 33

Ellen licked her dry lips and swallowed. Could she distract John in the other room, leaving herself and Gabriel alone with her purse? Her cell phone was on the bed next to him, in the front zippered pouch.

"Could I get some water? My throat's dry."

He didn't respond in the way she'd hoped. "Get up. Pick up that purse."

Heart sinking, she stood and snatched up her purse. Hit him with it? It wasn't as heavy as it typically was. Under normal circumstances, she'd have carried a novel and other sundries in it that would've given it a good heft, but she'd emptied it before going down to dinner.

"Drop the purse on the couch. You carry your phone in it. You won't get a chance to use it, and no one will track you with it. We'll leave it here in your hotel room where anyone searching for you will expect you to be."

Rhonda wouldn't worry until later when Ellen didn't show up for drinks. She glanced at the time. Just

210

after eight o'clock. How panicked would Rhonda get when Ellen didn't show and didn't answer her phone? How long before she notified the police? And what if Max was in on it? He'd prevent her from calling anyone.

Ellen set the purse on the couch.

"Get your bottle of water. Lover boy should be awake soon, and we'll go for a drive. We'll take your car."

"The keys are in my purse."

"Get your water. I'll get the keys."

She went to the fridge and retrieved a bottle of water. Twisting off the cap, she took a swig and then put the cap back on. John stood in front of the couch, one hand holding the gun in her general direction and the other awkwardly unzipping her purse. Tempted to tell him she'd get the keys, Ellen bit her lip. If she said anything, he'd likely do the opposite of what she suggested.

Her cell phone sounded, the ringtone Rhonda's.

Ellen took an involuntary step toward the couch to pick up the phone but stopped and held her breath, her gaze riveted on John.

***

When Gabriel first returned to consciousness, he heard Ellen's voice, and at first, his spirits rose. She'd found him. Everything was okay. He was about to open his eyes when he heard John's answering voice. Gabriel's stomach dropped, and he kept his eyes closed. He wasn't sure how that helped them, but anything that deprived John of knowledge of a change in circumstances felt like a win.

Gabriel took stock and mentally listed what he knew: one wrist was chained, probably to the headboard; his head ached and he felt like shit; Ellen sat on the bed beside him, her hand in his; John stood near the bed, and he likely held the gun he carried on Ellen.

After John had burst into the hotel suite, he'd forced Gabriel at gunpoint to drink a glass of juice, which likely had a drug in it since that was the last thing Gabriel recalled before awakening with Ellen on the bed.

Now, the two were in the other room, giving Gabriel precious time alone.

He opened his eyes and immediately felt in his pocket for his penknife. Still there. Not much of a weapon but not nothing.

"Hey!" John's voice startled Gabriel, and his heart skipped a beat, but the other man had shouted at Ellen. "I can't find the damn keys. You get them. Don't do anything stupid. I swear I'll shoot you dead and go to plan B. I'll hold your phone while you do that. Wouldn't want you alerting anyone with an accidental emergency call now, would we?"

Quietly, Gabriel shifted so he sat on the bed with his feet on the floor. No sudden moves or John would get twitchy. As long as the two remained in the living room, they couldn't see into the bedroom. Gabriel stood up. As he did, the cuff on his wrist rattled, and he froze.

"What's taking so fucking long?" The rage in John's voice, his foul language, almost had Gabriel shouting at the man.

"I've got them. See?" Ellen said, and keys rattled.

"Put them on the coffee table and take this key. I

want you to free Gabe and wake him. He should be out of it by now. We've got to get this show on the road."

Gabriel glanced from the bed to the doorway. The door was too far from the bed for him to ambush John as he returned to the room, and that kind of stunt could get himself and Ellen both shot.

"Hey, Gabe, you awake?" John chuckled. "Your girlfriend joined the party."

What should he do now?

"Move it. I don't have time for this shit." John continued to harangue Ellen. "I'm right behind you. One false move and I'll blow your stupid head off."

"I'm going." Ellen's voice was close.

Gabriel hurriedly lay down again and pretended to sleep. *Please, Ellen, play along or we're dead.*

Ellen stepped into the room and strode to the bed.

Gabriel stirred as though just waking up. "Do as he says. It'll be all right." Gabriel glanced at John, who hovered a few metres behind Ellen. "We'll get through this."

CHAPTER 34

Ellen approached the bed cautiously. When she sat down, the mattress shifted, and his warm body pressed against her thigh, offering a bit of physical reassurance.

She removed the handcuff from Gabriel's wrist, but when she went to set the key on the night table, John ordered her to take the cuff off the bed and hand it and the key over. She did as he bid, silently apologizing to Gabriel with her eyes for their predicament.

If only she'd noticed the missing "Do not disturb" sign. But if she had, wouldn't she have assumed Gabriel had removed it when he entered the room? Her guilt eased a fraction.

She helped the man she loved sit and then stand.

"Move it." John waved the gun at them, indicating they should go out into the living room.

"You lead and walk us to where you parked the car," he told Gabriel. "I'll escort the lady. One stupid move and she's dead. Got it?"

Expression grim, Gabriel said, "Understood."

John shielded the gun with Ellen's body and his

leather jacket, one arm draped over her shoulder. "Play along, babe, or I'll kill him after I kill you. Then, I'll kill anyone else you alert."

"Okay." She didn't know what else to say. Her mind raced, considering options. Two against one. Surely, they could stop him. Neither she nor Gabriel had a cell phone on them now. If they were to get out of this, it was up to them.

She halted before they reached the door. "I need to change my shoes."

"Quit stalling." John gave her a shove, and she stumbled, exaggerating the move by falling to her knees.

"I can't walk in these heels. Let me put flats on."

He hesitated, but in the end, he waved the gun in a random direction and said, "Hurry up."

Ellen put on a pair of running shoes she pulled from the closet next to the exit, moving quickly to tie them up before he stopped her. She had other shoes in there, dressier, which would've made more sense with the blouse and slacks she wore, but the sportier shoes would give her an edge if an opportunity to escape appeared.

They left the suite and headed for the elevator, John sticking so close to Ellen his breath tickled her cheek. She focused her gaze on Gabriel, setting him in her memory and her heart. If they were to die, she'd savour his presence now.

The elevator was empty when the doors opened, but as they passed the various floors, people got on. When they reached the lobby, everyone except their little group of three left. They carried on to the parking level, and Gabriel led them to their rental car.

John forced Gabriel to settle into the driver's seat

and made Ellen sit in the front passenger seat while he sat directly behind her. He insisted they all buckle up, more so they wouldn't attract police attention than to keep them safe in case of a crash. Something rustled. A scarf was yanked down over her head and tightened around her neck. As she struggled, it squeezed.

"Hold still or you'll strangle," John shouted, and when Gabriel made a move toward Ellen, he hollered, "Back off or I'll blow her head apart."

Gabriel settled, though his face was red with rage and he gripped the steering wheel with white-knuckled fists. Ellen, tears streaming down her face, went still. John adjusted the noose around her neck, the scarf tugging as he did something with it.

When all movement stopped, John said, "Keep still, Ellen, and you'll be fine. It's insurance so lover boy doesn't slam on the brakes or cause an accident to try to save your asses. You do that, champ, and she'll hang herself. Now, let's go."

The engine roared to life, and Gabriel eased the car from the parking spot. With John directing them, they drove to the highway leading to the desert. They'd barely gone a mile when John's cell phone buzzed.

"Keep your mouths shut. Wouldn't want this gun to blow Ellen's brains out." He answered the call. "Yeah? No, taking a little side trip to the Bellagio … a woman I met … Where's Rhonda? So, tag along … No, I'll see you in the morning. Don't wait up." He ended the call and tossed the phone on the seat beside him.

"You had plans with your girlfriend tonight."

When Ellen remained silent, he swatted her head. "Answer me when I talk to you."

"Yes, we had plans."

216

"Guess she'll assume you stood her up. Too bad."

"Yes." Ellen didn't know what else to say. Did he expect her to have a conversation with him? Unless he pressed her for details, she refused to reveal them. When he said nothing else, Ellen assumed he'd let the matter drop. Inside, she prayed for Rhonda to overreact when no one showed up to meet her for drinks.

A half hour later, all Ellen could see zooming past them were buttes, mesas, rocks, scrub, and desert sand. It crossed her mind that the car likely had a GPS on it, and it could be traced if they disappeared. If Rhonda grew suspicious, maybe she'd call the police. But the more Ellen thought about it, the more she understood it was too late for that. Even if Rhonda called the police this second, she'd have no reason to give them for starting a hunt right now. By the time the authorities concluded something was wrong, she and Gabriel would be dead.

After another fifteen minutes, John ordered Gabriel to pull off the road and drive into the desert. "Sorry I had to drag you along for this, Gabe, but forensics are pretty good these days, and they'd know if you died before she did. Plus, you need to be behind the wheel to drive her out here."

Tears leaked from Ellen's eyes, and she couldn't hold them back. This couldn't be how they ended. They'd never said "I love you" to one another. She reached out a hand and groped for any contact with Gabriel. Her fingers skimmed his thigh, and he took one hand off the steering wheel to clasp them.

"Both hands on the wheel, asshole," John immediately shouted.

Gabriel gave her hand a quick squeeze and released

her.

They drove over uneven ground, manoeuvring around boulders, scrub, bushes, and holes in the ground until no flat land remained.

"Slow down here," John ordered. "Another few metres. Perfect. Stop."

Something metallic rattled. "Give me the car keys."

Gabriel put the car into park and turned off the engine. He passed the keys back to John.

"Cuff yourself to the steering wheel." He passed a set of handcuffs to Gabriel. Moonlight glinted off the cuffs as he snapped one onto a wrist and the other onto the steering wheel.

The scarf around Ellen's neck eased, and John looped it back over her heard. Unconsciously, she ran her hands through her hair, snagging her finger on a bobby pin. She slipped it from her hair and hid it in her hand, not sure what she'd do with it. She tucked it under her so John wouldn't see she had something in her hand.

"Get out, Ellen."

She shook with terror. This was where he'd kill her.

"Let her go, John. You don't have to do this. Just let her go."

John ignored Gabriel's final attempt to save Ellen and said, "She owes me. I went out with her, and she never once let me fuck her. Not once. We're going to have some fun, and then I'll shoot her in the head because that's what she deserves. Get out of the car, Ellen."

"Don't touch her!" Gabriel struggled with the cuffs as if he could slip his hand out of it.

When John turned his head to look, Ellen leaped from the car and ran.

CHAPTER 35

I'm not running away.

Ellen ran, and as she ran, she zigzagged—at least, she zigzagged in what she interpreted the word to mean. She'd read that if you're running from a person with a gun, you had to zigzag so they couldn't nail you as easily. But she worried that she'd zig when she should zag and run straight into the bullet.

When the shot rang out behind her, she changed course again, praying she wasn't heading into its path. Enough time passed and she concluded he'd missed her. So, she ran and zigged and zagged and told herself she wasn't running away—not from Gabriel.

She had to escape, or neither one of them would get away. Gabriel was cuffed to the steering wheel, so it was up to her. Her mind rambled in a frenzied attempt to organize her thoughts, and all it did was make her heart pound and her breath hitch and her lungs ache.

John shouted at her to stop, to get back here—as though she'd do anything he told her to. She'd rather die in the cold desert than give him the satisfaction of letting him kill her, especially since he'd made it clear he had rape on his mind first. But his advantage was that he had Gabriel. Did John believe she wouldn't abandon Gabriel? If he did, she was done. All John needed to do was wait for her to come back to the car. Unless Gabriel had seen the gift she'd left for him. The hairpin. Her hope was he'd seen it and all John's plans had suddenly turned to shit.

***

When Ellen ran for it, Gabriel cheered internally. He didn't call out to encourage her, afraid it might make her stop and turn around. If he'd had the chance to run, he'd have taken it as well. She wasn't abandoning him. She didn't abandon people—that was his MO.

In the frantic moments after she tore off into the desert with John racing after her, firing uselessly into the dark—*go ahead, asshole, and use up all your bullets*—Gabriel wasted a few precious seconds tugging at the handcuff around his wrist. Rationality eventually caught up to panic and emotion, and he searched the vehicle for anything he could use to break or unlock the cuffs. He tried the glove box first and found only documents related to the rental. Nothing to help him there.

As he turned his attention away from the dashboard area, his gaze fell on the front passenger seat, and he spotted the bobby pin. He almost missed it in the dark—would have if the moon hadn't spilled enough light for him to catch the glint of metal. He curled his fingers around it and clasped it tightly.

He'd never had to open a pair of handcuffs with a hairpin before—never expected to have to and not under such pressure. From outside, gunshots rang out and shouts carried on the air, but the shouts, thankfully, were all enraged curses from John, which meant he hadn't caught Ellen.

As long as John focused on her, they had a chance if Gabriel could escape these cuffs. He didn't know what he was doing but intuited he'd have to straighten out the hairpin and get those plastic nubs off the ends. Unbending it was easy enough, but when it came to getting the plastic off the end, he had to use his teeth, and all this took time. He slipped the pin into the lock and realized after some fiddling that he needed to bend the end. He braced the pin inside the lock and pressed.

This was taking too long. Gabriel glanced nervously out into the darkness and could no longer see John. Good news and bad news.

Please don't catch her. Ellen, run and don't stop. It was a prayer, in a way. He didn't say "God" and he didn't bargain, but he meant both those things even if he considered himself an atheist. *Who'd have thought I'm actually agnostic?*

He twisted again, and this time, the bracelet on his wrist opened. He wasted another second or two recognizing he'd accomplished his goal, and then, he moved.

First, he checked the back seat. His reward was the cell phone John had left behind. Next, he threw open the car's door and leaped into the night, running in the direction opposite to the one Ellen had taken. He bypassed the first few boulders he came to and took shelter atop a rocky dune shielded by a bit of scrub brush and some boulders.

Gabriel called 911.

***

The farther Ellen ran from the vehicle, the more she feared getting lost in the desert and dying there. Still better than what John had planned, but she slowly started to rebel against that fate as well. And she still had to somehow save Gabriel, because at some point, John would decide to let nature take her and go back to murder the man who, in his mind, had set all this in motion.

She ducked behind the next boulder she came across and waited to see if John would catch up to her. All her focus went to calming her panting breath so as not to give away her hiding place, but every time she held her breath to tamp down the noise, she started panting again when she resumed breathing. At last, with great effort, she settled herself enough to breathe silently.

Now that she listened, the desert came alive. Wind swooshed, making a sound like cars speeding along a distant highway. The occasional bird call reached her ears, and she concluded it must be owls because what else would be out at night? As a city girl, the only nocturnal creatures she was familiar with were raccoons and the odd skunk. She strained to hear the sound of pursuing footsteps or heavy breathing, but none came. Where was he? Had he already turned back? Terror drove her to her feet, and she started to head back in the direction she'd come, but she stopped herself before she took too many steps.

Listen first. Look first. She had to coach herself, or she'd scream out Gabriel's name and get them both killed. Now that she wasn't running in a panic, the cold seeped into her bones, making her shiver. Her legs ached. The shoes might've been built for running, but she wasn't a runner, especially not across all this rock and sandstone.

Rocks loomed over her. In the daytime, the red rock formations must be breathtaking, but in the dark, she feared they hid either John or wildlife that wanted to attack and eat her. The wailing wind brought to mind ghosts, perhaps of those already secretly buried here. If John had his way, she'd join them soon.

The sirens, at first, were faint and background noise. When they finally registered in her brain, she jumped from her hiding place and slowly traced a path back in their direction. But she wasn't stupid. If she wanted to get to the police, John would want to get away from them if he was still on the loose. She didn't dare hope the approach of sirens meant Gabriel had caught John and called the police. Assuming could get her killed.

Ellen slowed her pace and walked in the direction she expected the rental car to be parked, squinting to try to discern headlights in the distance. This turned out to be a useless exercise since the rolling dunes made seeing any great distance impossible. Each time she reached the top of the next dune or rock formation, she turned a full 360 degrees to see if any lights displayed at all anywhere on the ground. After what she estimated was half an hour, she realized she was lost.

CHAPTER 36

Gabriel kept the connection to emergency services open so he could direct them to his location, but even so, they had to leave their vehicles farther out and search for him using flashlights. In the meantime, Gabriel's biggest concern remained John and whether he'd caught Ellen or would stumble on Gabriel before the police arrived. He heaved a sigh of relief when he spotted the beams of the searching lights approaching and ran to meet them. What he wasn't prepared for was for them to tell him he couldn't help them find Ellen.

"He's armed. He'll kill her. Or he'll use her as a hostage. Don't you get it?" Gabriel shouted at the sergeant. By this point, a canine unit had arrived, and they were already scouring the area. The officers taking part in the search had heavy-duty flashlights to help them cut through the dark.

The man grasped Gabriel by the upper arm and guided him to a nearby officer. "I understand more than you know, sir. We'll find her. Rhonda Miller already reported Ellen Haddigan missing, so we'd already started a search. The dogs will pick up the scent from the vehicle and track them both. A helicopter is on its way. It'll get colder before it gets warmer, and I can't stay here arguing with you." He turned to the officer. "Escort Mr. Duncan to the cruiser and wait there with him."

"At least let me wait at my car," Gabriel argued. "If he's going to try to get anywhere, it'll be back to my car."

The officer glanced at the sergeant, who shook his head.

"He's armed, as you pointed out. I won't allow a civilian to walk into danger. Go with the officer, Mr. Duncan, or I'll have him drive you back to the station. That cruiser is as close as I'll let you get to the action."

Gabriel grasped the sergeant's arm and said, "Find her. If anything happens to her ..." He shook his head. "I can't lose her."

"Don't worry. We'll find them."

Gabriel allowed the police officer to lead him to the cruiser to begin who knew how many minutes or hours of sitting and stewing. As they reached the cruiser, somewhere out in the desert, a gun fired.

***

The sound of the gunshot echoed off the dunes, and chunks blew off a boulder behind her. Ellen froze and then turned in the direction from which she thought it had come but saw nothing.

Oh, God, she never should've run. Now, she'd die out here in the desert without helping Gabriel. Why did she always run away from every problem? She should've—what? Stayed there to be raped and

225

murdered just to have John shoot Gabriel anyway? She should be grateful he'd fired. It gave her a direction to go, and the fact he hadn't fired again might mean it'd been a lucky shot. He had as much trouble seeing her in the dark as she did seeing him. If she could sneak up on him, she might ... She might get shot, that was what she might do. She shoved visions of wrestling the gun away from John and rescuing Gabriel from her head. She had to be smart.

She searched for a rock. *Because what you want is to bring a rock to a gunfight.* Even so, it would be better than nothing.

When she found a suitably sized rock, she crept in the direction from where the shot had fired. Tempted as she was to move quickly, she feared stumbling across John in the dark. He could be hiding behind a boulder or bush. She strained her ears to catch the slightest sound, whether of John or a wild animal.

In the distance came the mechanical whoosh of a helicopter approaching. When she turned toward it, she saw its white strobe lights and red navigation lights moving in her direction.

Relief flooded through her. The helicopter could mean Gabriel had escaped and called the police. Ellen jumped up and down and waved her arms.

Please, this way. I'm here.

An arm grabbed her from behind and squeezed her into a hard body. "Got ya!"

John.

Her fist tightened around the rock, and she stomped on his foot while jabbing an elbow in his gut. When his arm around her loosened, she spun around and clobbered him in the face with the rock. Blood spurted from his nose. She snatched the gun from his hand and hurled it into the darkness.

She waved her arms, ran toward the helicopter, and jumped and screamed her desperation.

A spotlight from the huge bird flared on and pinned her, and a voice boomed out, "Stay where you are. Put your hands in the air."

She obliged but spun around to make sure John wasn't gaining on her. He was a faint blob, on his knees at the periphery of the searchlight. A police dog had him frozen in place, and two police officers had guns levelled at him. Ellen's body shook with relief and shock and cold. She'd survived. Now to find Gabriel.

***

After spending most of the night getting checked out by paramedics and talking to the police, Ellen and Gabriel entered their new hotel room, relieved the nightmare was over. The police had cordoned off their original suite, gathering evidence against John, and the hotel manager had kindly relocated their possessions to another suite as soon as investigators allowed it. Since the room was an upgrade and none of their belongings had been lost in the shuffle, Ellen and Gabriel welcomed the change.

"I don't think I'd feel comfortable staying there after everything that happened," Ellen said as she stripped off her clothes and dropped them, piece by piece, on the floor. "I need a bath." She shivered, feeling as if she'd never be able to get the chill of the desert out of her bones.

When Gabriel kept silent, she stopped and stood naked before him in the dim light from the single lamp she'd lit on the night table next to her side of the king bed. One hand still clutched the panties she'd removed.

"What is it?"

He remained motionless, silhouetted in the doorway by the light spilling in from the living room. His brow was furrowed, and his lips turned down in a frown.

"Ellen," he began, but he fell silent. His expression grew anguished, and it sent spikes of fear through her heart.

Would he end their relationship now while she stood shivering and vulnerable before him?

"For God's sake, what is it?" The words came out more frightened than she'd intended, but the truth was, he terrified her. She'd expected never to live through the night, and they had. Now, all she wanted was a bath and Gabriel's arms around her, warm in their bed.

What had he been thinking while she ran from their would-be murderer? Did he think she'd left him to die? Was now really the time to discuss it? She wasn't ready for that.

He moved into the room then and reached her side in two long strides.

"I know you're tired." He rubbed his hands along her arms. "And cold."

He grabbed the terry robe she'd placed on the bed and put it on her, helping her slide her arms into it as if she were a child. "If I don't get this out, though ... How can you pretend nothing happened?"

"I'm not pretending," she said, astounded. "We survived. I'm relieved we did. I'm trying to take things one step at a time." She buried her face in her hands. "I'm so cold. It was so cold out there. I was thinking a bath would warm me up. Was that selfish?"

Had something happened to him that she'd

overlooked? She could be oblivious to others when she was uncomfortable. Why didn't she think about how he felt? What he'd experienced?

He drew her into his arms, and she relaxed a little but then remembered how alone and abandoned she'd felt after their first night together when they'd parted ways for three long years. Yet, he'd had his reasons, and she understood them now. She had to trust what he wanted to say now wouldn't destroy her life. Again.

"Of course not. I need to tell you, Ellen, I can't lose you ever again. This isn't a reaction to a near-miss murder attempt on our lives. I lost you for three years. Tonight, I almost lost you forever. I can't bear the thought of a life without you in it." He tilted her chin up with one finger and pressed his lips gently to hers.

After a moment, he broke the kiss. "I don't have a ring to give you, but if you promise to marry me, I'll buy you a stunning one. I'm not going to London. We're staying here, and I'm going to do what I should've done all along: sell BRI, which I never should've bought, and buy a restaurant. I love you, Ellen. Marry me."

Her breath hitched as she choked back a sob. "I was so terrified that if John stopped chasing me he'd go back and kill you. I couldn't have faced a life without you either." She smiled at him. "But a restaurant? Are you sure?"

"I've never done what I wanted, always tried to please my old man. My brother can run the company— he's always wanted to. I have to chase my dream, not his." He covered her face with kisses, muttering, "Tell me you'll back me. You'll marry me and be my controller. We'll do this together."

"Is that really what you want?"

He pulled away and tilted her chin up. "I want to marry you. I love you."

"And the restaurant? You want that too?"

"I thought we'd die tonight, and after regretting I hadn't married you three years ago, I regretted never following my dream. Not my father's—mine. Life's too short to spend it building his empire. He has other people who'll help him do that. I have to try. Tell me you'll help me. Tell me you'll marry me."

"Oh, Gabe, I love you too. Yes, I'll marry you." His excitement infected her, and she envisioned the two of them working together, married, happy. She grinned. "On one condition."

He tilted his head to the side and gave her a dubious look. "What's that?"

"I get to help you pick the ring."

CHAPTER 37

A rose-gold band with honeycombed diamonds and a round solitaire diamond caught Ellen's eye in the Bloor-Yorkville jewellery shop through which she and Gabriel browsed. They'd had lunch nearby, and after two months of searching high and low for the perfect engagement ring, she thought perhaps they'd finally found the right one. She waved to the salesperson, a tall brunette with sleek, glossy hair and a trim figure under her tailored navy suit.

"May I try this one, please?" Ellen's cheeks flushed with excitement, and she had a sudden urge to dance and spin around the store. *This is the one.*

Beside her, Gabriel laughed, a deep hearty chuckle that sent more shivers of excitement up her spine. He draped an arm around her waist and pulled her in close as the saleswoman slipped the ring out from below the glass counter and offered it to Ellen. She accepted it and slid it on her finger.

The fit was slightly loose but not so much the diamond didn't sit right in the middle of her finger as long as she kept a steadying thumb pressed against the band. She held her hand out and studied the result from different angles.

"It's beautiful," she breathed. "Gabe, isn't this beautiful?"

"Everything looks beautiful on you." He kissed her cheek. "But this one matches the sparkle in your eyes the most."

"Oh, yuck. Listen to us. We've become sappy and syrupy. I swore I'd never sound like this." But she grinned at him to show him she loved it. His words warmed her insides, and his gaze, always affectionate and kind, said more than mere words ever could. Yet the surge of joy and gratitude evaporated as her thoughts turned to Zach and to Rhonda and Max.

Zach had sold his condo to pay back what Francesca had stolen. Three conspirators had been in on it, each playing a role in the thefts and in funnelling the money to accounts they held. John had goaded Francesca into it, and she'd pulled in Katrina. While the guilty should be punished, Zach continued to pay for what his wife had done.

Rhonda and Max were also collateral damage: they'd split up, and Rhonda swore she'd never trust another man. She insisted Max had betrayed her—had betrayed Ellen as well by exposing her to John. Nothing Ellen said in his defence swayed Rhonda. She ended the relationship and insisted it was for the best.

"John almost killed you," Rhonda had explained to Ellen the night before. "Who you hang out with says a lot about you."

"Max didn't know. The police investigated. They cleared him."

Rhonda shook her head. "Max planned to partner

with him. That's why they were at the convention. How could he have not known?"

Ellen had no answer to that. Rhonda had a point. The two men had been best friends, as close as Ellen and Rhonda were. If Rhonda were involved in something illegal, Ellen was sure she'd at least suspect. And murder? No way could her friend hide a side of her capable of committing murder.

"What's wrong?" Gabriel's voice drew Ellen back to the moment.

"Nothing. I'm fine."

But he gave her a squeeze, indicating he refused to accept the response. "Tell me. Is it the price?" He checked the sticker in the case. "It's a little more than we agreed to spend, but for the perfect ring, I'm willing to go over budget."

She shook her head. "No. I'm quite happy to let you go over budget."

Both smiled at that.

"Then, what is it?" His expression showed so much concern she had a moment of guilt for causing it.

"Rhonda and Max." She sighed. "I'm sorry. I can't help feeling sad at how their relationship ended." She brightened at a sudden thought. "I know exactly what to do."

Gabriel frowned. When he spoke, his tone was emphatic. "You're not interfering in someone's love life."

"No, I'm going to get her a gift." She turned her gaze on the saleswoman. "Do you have any rose quartz jewellery?"

"Sure," the woman replied and strode to another counter. "I'll bring you a few to look at."

Ellen lifted her chin so she could gaze into Gabriel's

eyes. "Rose quartz attracts love. Rhonda gave one to me for my birthday. I'm returning the favour." No strings attached. No expectation of reciprocation. She could get used to this gift-giving thing.

"It's a nice gesture." He tilted his face down and brushed his lips against hers. "She'll love it, although I'm dubious that the crystal will have any effect on her love life."

"Trust me, this will draw love into her life," Ellen replied. "Who knows? Maybe she and Max will find their way back to each other. I found you again, didn't I?"

The sales clerk had arranged three necklaces on the counter, each with a silver chain and a polished quartz pendant. Ellen selected the one with the pink stone entangled in a love knot. "This one," she said emphatically. She smiled to herself, and when she spoke, excitement coloured her voice. "Rhonda will meet the love of her life."

"I'm sure she will," Gabriel replied. "You make a gorgeous cupid." He scooped her to him again for one more kiss.

When they stepped onto the sidewalk outside the store fifteen minutes later, Ellen had a receipt for the engagement ring tucked in her wallet. The jeweller would resize it, and they'd pick it up in a week or so. The necklace for Rhonda she'd tucked into her purse. She couldn't wait to give her friend the gift. Even if the crystal didn't bring Rhonda her true love, it would show her she had a true friend.

SAMPLE CHAPTER: *INJURY*

Eyes closed, sheet covering her face, Daniella Grayson groped for the phone and dragged the receiver to her ear. "Hello?"

"This is Tobey Ames from TNN, Miss Grayson. Do you have any comment on last night's arrest of your mother?"

Were she not so hung over, Dani would've bolted up. Instead, she drew her legs to her chest, assuming the fetal position. "No comment." The hand that held the phone dropped to the bed. Thumb probing for the "End" button, she found it and disconnected the call.

The phone rang again as she contemplated whom to call first. This time, she let it go to voice-mail. The machine in the living room clicked on after the third ring. The message and beep played, and John Madden, her manager, came on, sounding intense. "Dani. Are you screening? Pick up. I've been getting calls about your mother ..."

Dani sat this time, resting her aching head on bent knees, and answered. "What's going on, John? Tobey

Ames just called, asking about my mother's arrest."

"I don't know the details yet. They're accusing your mother of killing your father twenty years ago. You would have been what, then? Five?"

Silence. Dani tried to understand what John was telling her. "My father left us when I was five." Dani's mouth went dry, and her hands and feet grew cold. "Lilli was a bitch from hell." Nausea threatened and her spine prickled as she processed the awful news. *Could it be possible? Oh, God.* "She's capable of it. If they've arrested her for killing Daddy, she probably did it." An edge of hysteria had crept into her voice.

"Listen," John said. "Don't answer the phone or open the door until I get there. I'll call the lawyer on my way over, and we'll figure this thing out. There must be a mistake."

Dani said goodbye to John and hung up the phone. She shivered as she slipped out from under the covers and got out of bed. A glance at the clock on her nightstand showed seven-twenty in the morning. No wonder she felt like shit—she'd just gotten *into* bed at four-thirty, helped up to her apartment once again by her trusty chauffeur, what's his name? She always had trouble remembering. Oh, yeah, Cope.

Good looking as hell, but too young for Dani's tastes, and her employee, so she barely gave him a second glance. But he was kind and helpful and made sure she got home safely no matter how drunk she was.

Dani grabbed her bathrobe and snuggled her naked body into the warm terry cloth. As she slid her feet into a pair of slippers, the phone rang again. She returned to her nightstand and disconnected the phone. It continued to ring in the living room until the machine kicked in.

She listened for the caller's voice.

"Hello, Miss Grayson. It's Mark Rutherford of ASN. John Madden suggested you give me an exclusive interview. I'd love to hear your side of the story. Please call me back at ..."

Dani shook her head in disgust while Rutherford recited his phone number. She pulled the plug on the living room phone as well. Anyone she'd want to talk to could call her cell.

She sank onto the couch, switched on the TV, and clicked over to the news channel. An eternity seemed to pass before the stories cycled to the one about her mother. Finally, the newscaster returned to the headline news.

A somber Toby Ames faced the camera, eyes filled with compassion. "Ms. Lillian Capshaw, mother of Oscar-nominated actress Daniella Grayson, was arrested last night in her apartment in Toronto on charges of first degree murder in the death of her husband Paul Grayson. Grayson's skeletal remains were discovered yesterday morning in a capped well at a Sharon, Ontario residence once rented by the family. Ms. Capshaw was taken into custody late last night."

Dani's childhood home flashed on the screen behind the reporter. Plywood covered the windows, and two police cars sat in the driveway. Video footage of Dani appeared on the screen next, showing her exiting a limousine.

The newscaster continued in voiceover. "Miss Grayson, seen here arriving at the premiere of her movie, the Academy Award-winning best picture *Injury*, lives in Los Angeles and has not commented on last night's events. We will update you as the story progresses."

Dani flicked to a channel that focused more on entertainment news. After a few minutes, her photo appeared behind the news anchor, and he gave the same spiel as Ames had though without the premiere clip.

The footage then switched to a taped interview with Gregory Henderson, caught leaving a restaurant with a date. Dani swallowed past a lump in her throat and hugged herself, terrified of what Henderson might say.

Always an attention hog, Henderson leaned toward the female reporter and into the microphone. "No, I haven't talked to Dani. She's not speaking to me these days."

Dani noted the slight slur in his speech. Henderson's arm rested around the shoulders of a gorgeous blonde, who looked delighted to be with him, getting her fifteen minutes of fame.

"Did you meet Lilli Capshaw when you were dating Miss Grayson?"

"No ma'am." Henderson swayed and steadied himself by leaning on his date. "Dani kept me all to herself." He looked into the camera. "Call me, sweetheart. I'm here for you, baby."

The date lost her look of delight.

After a few more inane questions from the reporter and more slurred responses from Henderson, the interview wrapped up.

What an ass. Dani switched off the television, recalling the premiere. She'd stepped out of the limousine and had smiled for the cameras while voices of people she didn't know had cried out for her to look their way.

She hooked her arm through Greg Henderson's and hoped her four-inch heels wouldn't catch on the red carpet. "Greg," she whispered, "don't let go of my arm."

He smiled at her. "Relax, baby. I've got you covered."

Dani loved tall men. At five-foot-ten, she usually looked most men in the eyes—looked down on them, let's be honest—especially in four-inch heels. Henderson was the perfect height for her, and their chemistry on screen and high-profile romance off screen had helped make *Injury* the hit of the season.

She tried to get in front of the cameras as much as possible and had worked hard at looking particularly stunning for that premiere. Her body-hugging gown had shown off her slender figure. She'd let her long, dark hair hang loose in a wild and carefree way that took hours with a curling iron to achieve.

Maybe my father is watching this, she'd thought, as she always did when she put herself on display in public. It's *why* she put herself on display in public.

Daddy's never seen me. All those times, I thought he'd see me and feel sorry he left us, and he wasn't even alive.

The doorbell rang. *John.*

She unfurled from the couch and waited for him to enter. When the door didn't open, she walked over, reached for the deadbolt, and then remembered John's warning to not open the door. She checked the peephole. Nothing there. If that was John, he wouldn't be hiding. She waited. The doorbell rang again, but whoever was there took pains not to be seen.

Dani left the door, went to her room, and opened her closet. *There'll be a media feeding frenzy. What am I going to wear?*

Did it matter? Yes, she supposed it did, but it felt strange to know that her father wasn't out there somewhere perhaps noticing her and thinking about contacting her.

At eighteen, she'd tried to find him, to ask him why he'd turned his back on her. She could understand that he'd want to escape controlling, abusive, obsessive Lilli. Dani herself had moved out of her mother's home at sixteen. But Dani was a child when her dad had disappeared, and she'd taken the rejection and ensuing lack of contact personally.

The knocking on the door penetrated her thoughts. *How'd that asshole get into the building?* Multiple fists pounded the door, she realized. More than one asshole was out there in the hall stalking her. Then she heard voices arguing, demanding. She hopped back into bed, pulled the covers under her chin, and waited.

A key rattling in the door told her John had arrived. Dani sighed and slid out of bed. Peering out of her bedroom, she waited for him to step inside. John, handsome, rugged, older. But assertive, protective, kind. She itched to touch him.

Would he sleep with her now she was over twenty-one? It'd been five years since she'd tested those waters. When she'd first hired him to be her manager, she'd thrown herself at him.

She'd almost fired him when he'd rejected her, then had decided she didn't give a shit after all. One by one, she'd seduced his associates, until she'd gotten it out of her system. The older men had been eager to accept the offer of her young body.

When John had complained, like he had any right to say anything about whom she fucked, she'd told him to butt out. He'd almost quit on her then, and she'd had to beg and plead and promise the moon to keep him as her manager. Fear of him abandoning her reined in her reckless, wanton behavior, and she'd battled to keep him in her life.

They'd had a holy alliance since then, focusing on her career, which had skyrocketed. She'd kept her attraction to him locked away, taking it out only in the darkest of nights when she took comfort from and pleasured herself on thoughts of him.

But now that ache for him was back, fierce, hot. Dani slid a hand down her robe and loosened the knot on the belt at her waist. The robe parted slightly, exposing her body in a thin, vertical line of curves and shadows. Her nipples hardened, and she parted her lips.

She tilted her head to the side and watched John struggle to shut the door as hands holding microphones jammed themselves into the opening, and voices shouted her name. John pushed against the door, and a man cried out in pain. The arms disappeared, and the door slammed shut.

"Don't worry, Dani. I've alerted security. They'll be gone soon," John said, his back to her.

The normality of seeing him there shook her back to reality, and she closed the robe. When he turned to her, she faced him head on. "John." Her voice caught in her throat, and his name came out low and throaty, but it was grief, not lust that did it. "What happened to my father?"

ABOUT THE AUTHOR

Val Tobin lives in Newmarket, Ontario with her husband, Bob, and Scully, their cat. She spends her days writing, reading, and searching for the perfect butter tart.

CONNECT WITH VAL TOBIN

Facebook: www.facebook.com/valtobinauthor
Twitter: twitter.com/valandbob
Blog: bobandval.wordpress.com/
BookBub: bookbub.com/authors/val-tobin
Web Site: valtobin.com
ALLi: allianceindependentauthors.org/members/val-tobin/profile/

OTHER BOOKS BY VAL TOBIN

Fiction

Paranormal Sci-Fi Thrillers

The Valiant Chronicles Series

Earthbound (prequel): A spirit becomes earthbound after refusing to cross over in order to solve her murder and prevent more deaths, some of which might be predestined.

The Experiencers (book one): A black-ops assassin atones for his brutal past by helping an alien abductee escape capture.

A Ring of Truth (Book Two): A rogue assassin triggers an apocalypse when he attempts to rescue a group of alien abductees.

The Valiant Chronicles books are also available as a complete set in e-book and paperback.

Romantic Suspense

Injury: A young actress at the height of her career has her personal life turned upside down when a horrifying family secret makes front-page news.

Gillian's Island: A socially anxious divorcée confronts her greatest fears when she's forced to sell her island home and falls for the dashing new owner.

About Three Authors: Poison Pen: Three wannabe authors suffering from various mental disorders find love in unexpected places when they interfere in the investigation of a colleague's murder.

Forever Young: You Again: Complications arise when an accounting tech is assigned her former lover as a client and his company's previous financial controller is found dead.

Paranormal Romance

Walk-In: A young psychic woman fights an attraction to a handsome but sceptical novelist while she battles a power-hungry sorcerer determined to make her his next conquest.

Horror Suspense

The Hunted: A Storm Lake Story: A monster hunter revisits her terrifying past while helping a reporter uncover the origins of Storm Lake's creatures. A stand-alone sequel to the short story "Storm Lake," *The Hunted* takes place twelve years later.

Urban Fantasy

Tales from the Unmasqued World Series

The Fool: New Beginnings (book one): A newly divorced woman suffering a midlife crisis gets involved in the search for a missing half-vampire teen.

The Magician: Infinity's End (book two): After getting expelled for setting a demon loose on campus, a student mage searches for the real culprit and finds his troubles have only just begun.

The High Priestess: Persephone's Return (book three): Stuck in the spirit world, Jaycie struggles to find a way out. But others want to keep her there forever. Will she make it out of Hades alive?

Nonfiction

Angel Words by Doreen Virtue and Grant Virtue
Val contributed a story to Doreen and Grant Virtue's *Angel Words: Visual Evidence of How Words Can Be Angels in Your Life*

www.ingramcontent.com/pod-product-compliance
Lightning Source LLC
Chambersburg PA
CBHW011434240626
47153CB00011B/2983